WENTWORTH HALL

WENTWORTH HALL

ABBY GRAHAME

SIMON & SCHUSTER BFYR

NEW YORK LONDON TORONTO SYDNEY NEW DELHI

SIMON & SCHUSTER BFYR

An imprint of Simon & Schuster Children's Publishing Division
1230 Avenue of the Americas, New York, New York 10020

For information about special discounts for bulk purchases, please contact Simon &
Schuster Special Sales at 1-866-506-1949 or business@simonandschuster.com.
The Simon & Schuster Speakers Bureau can bring authors to your live event. For more
information or to book an event, contact the Simon & Schuster Speakers Bureau at
1-866-248-3049 or visit our website at www.simonspeakers.com.
Also available in a SIMON & SCHUSTER BFYR hardcover edition
Book design by Lucy Ruth Cummins
The text for this book is set in Goudy Old Style.
Manufactured in the United States of America
First SIMON & SCHUSTER BFYR paperback edition January 2013
2 4 6 8 10 9 7 5 3 1
The Library of Congress has cataloged the hardcover edition as follows:
Grahame, Abby.
Wentworth Hall / Abby Grahame.
p. cm.
Summary: In 1912 England, eighteen-year-old Maggie Darlington returns from
France to learn that her father hopes to restore the family fortunes through her marriage
and his guardianship of two orphaned teens, but scandalous satires in the newspaper
threaten to spoil his plans and reveal the family's many secrets.
ISBN 978-1-4424-5196-4 (hc)
[1. Family life—England—Fiction. 2. Social classes—Fiction. 3. Interpersonal
relations—Fiction. 4. Secrets—Fiction. 5. Great Britain—History—George V, 1910–
1936—Fiction.] I. Title.
PZ7.G7587Wen 2012
[Fic]—dc23
2011051461
ISBN 978-1-4424-5197-1 (pbk)
ISBN 978-1-4424-5198-8 (eBook)

To Julia Maguire and Zareen Jaffery,
with thanks for all their creative and editorial ideas

WENTWORTH HALL

~ Chapter One

MAGGIE DARLINGTON ROLLED OVER IN bed and squinted into the sunlight pouring through the lace curtains of her bedroom window. As if suddenly realizing where she was, she groaned, spread her fingers wide, and placed both hands over her face. She wordlessly cursed the brilliant sunshine and bemoaned her return to Wentworth Hall, sliding deeper under her floral eiderdown quilt and soft, voluminous bed covers.

If she were in Paris—as she had been only two weeks earlier—the red velvet drapes would still be drawn and she'd be permitted to sleep until noon—at least. To think, she had looked forward to coming home. She had really believed life would return to normal after her year away in France. How wrong she had been.

But, like it or not, she was back in Sussex now, and Nora, her ladies maid, had already begun their morning ritual, slipping silently into her room only a few hours after dawn to draw aside the heavy damask window coverings. It was Maggie's father, Lord Arthur Darlington's, none-too-subtle way of rousing the household for the day. Her father loved Wentworth Hall, and felt his entire family should share his affection. Never mind the fact that there wasn't much to *do* at the house if you were a lady. Other than read in the library. Or practice sewing in the parlor. Or have tea with her younger sister, Lila. Despite eighteen years of doing just that, Maggie had yet to grow fond of those activities.

Dropping her hands down by her sides as if in surrender, she realized it was no use trying to go back to sleep. She had already spent the last few weeks claiming the journey had exhausted her. If she couldn't get back to normal exactly, she did have to find a new routine, a new "normal." And no better day than the present to get started.

She could hear the servants already up and about. Footsteps trundled down the hall, and the lingering homey smell of bacon was unmistakable. Probably a servant delivering Lady Darlington's breakfast. She was the only one Lord Darlington allowed the luxury of breakfast in the bedroom, and solely because Lady Beatrice Darlington had recently delivered him a second male heir. Meanwhile, said male heir was being cared for night and day by the French nanny they had brought back from Paris.

Although Maggie claimed to have developed a preference for the "continental breakfast" of pastry and dark coffee she'd been enjoying during the past year's stay in Nice and then Paris, this morning the idea of a good English "fry-up" had appeal.

Maggie tossed off the quilt, letting it slide to the floor, sat up, and stretched her lanky frame. Gathering her lush honey blond curls into a bundle, she twisted the hair into a topknot that would hold its form without the help of hairpins or a ribbon.

She lowered herself from her high four-poster bed, pulled a matching peignoir over the daring rose-colored satin nightgown her aunt had purchased for her on the Champs Élysées and crossed to the window.

Green hills dotted with trees rolled out for miles, and the stream's water sparkled in the distance. It called to mind the many hours she'd spent riding on those very grounds. She remembered laughing as she galloped faster and faster, scaring Michael, her groom, and forcing him to race after her. Once upon a time, Maggie had spent as many waking hours as possible out in those very fields, relishing the feel of the wind in her hair and the reckless abandon of pushing her favorite horse, Buckingham, to his limits.

But those days of girlish, *foolish*, behavior were over.

She stepped back when she saw Michael walking out of the stable with Lila's horse, Windsor. Maggie hadn't seen Michael since the day she left for the Continent, over a year ago. From this distance, he looked just as she remembered—broad shoulders, strong arms, and easy, self-assured gait. He'd always had a confidence about him, even when they were children. She caught sight of her reflection in the windowpane and wondered if he would notice any difference in her. Not that she planned to give him an opportunity to do so.

Maggie inspected her hazy appearance in the glass, not so much to admire it—though since childhood everyone had commented on what a pretty girl she was and she wasn't deaf to the praise—but rather to search for signs of change. Surely the experiences abroad had lent maturity to her features? Had the girlish sparkle left her brown eyes, replaced by a new worldliness?

There was a knock on the door. "Come in," Maggie responded, turning and crossing her room to take a seat at her vanity. She assumed Nora was returning to lay out her clothing.

"Pardon, mademoiselle."

Turning sharply toward the unexpected voice, Maggie took in the figure of petite, delicate Therese, nanny to newborn James.

"What is it, Therese?" Maggie's tone was colder than she had intended.

"Madame Darlington is still sleeping and I am not sure. . . . Shall I take baby James for a stroll this morning?" Therese inquired in her heavily accented English.

"Why would you ask me?" Maggie snapped. Seeing the bags under Therese's normally sparkling brown eyes made her regret her tone. Perhaps Therese was homesick for France. Or for her mother, who Maggie had learned had died only a year before, leaving Therese without any family in the world.

"I am sorry. I only thought—"

Feeling guilty for her peevishness, Maggie softened. "Please don't apologize. I only meant that James is not my responsibility. If Lady Darlington is still sleeping, ask my father to wake her."

Therese stepped back, almost recoiling from the very idea. "Oh, no," she said, hesitating. "I would never wish to bother Lord Darlington with such a matter."

"I don't see why not. I can't imagine what Lord Darlington could be doing that is more important."

"Right now he is addressing the staff," Therese told her.

Maggie sniffed with annoyance. "What's he bothering them about now?" Though it did explain why Nora wasn't there to help her dress. Maggie walked over to her wardrobe to select an outfit for herself.

"I am not certain. I was told it did not concern me." Therese tilted her head toward the open door. "Pardon, I must return to little James."

"Yes, yes, by all means, go," Maggie dismissed Therese with an absent wave and surveyed the many dresses in front of her. The less she saw of Therese—and baby James, for that matter—the better.

Before she'd selected the day's outfit, seventeen-year-old

Nora burst into the room, red-faced and frazzled. "Sorry, Miss Maggie. I was hoping you weren't up yet. His lordship was giving us a talk and I just slipped away quiet-like because I didn't want to leave you stranded here in your room with nothing to wear."

"Well, you needn't have worried, Nora. I'm perfectly capable of dressing myself. In fact, from now on let's just skip this dressing ritual. Really, it's so old-fashioned. What do you say?"

Nora bustled past Maggie and pulled a charcoal gray frock with a wide white bib collar from the wardrobe and laid it out across a love seat in the corner of the room. "Her ladyship would never hear of that!" Nora objected firmly. "It wouldn't be right."

Turning, hands on her hips, Nora looked Maggie up and down. "You're looking very *ooh-la-la* today. Very pretty nightgown, I dare say, but has your mother seen it?"

"I'm eighteen, Nora! I don't have to have my mother's permission for my nightgown."

"You got that in Paris, didn't you?" Nora guessed with an air of disapproval. "And I'll wager her Ladyship wasn't with you when you bought it."

"Nora!" Maggie scolded. She had known Nora for as long as she could remember and she wasn't about to be lectured to by the waifish, freckle-faced maid with whom she'd played as a child while Nora's mother cooked downstairs in the servants' quarters.

"Have it your own way," Nora gave in. "You always do, anyway." She pulled open a dresser drawer and selected a full-length slip, stockings, garters, a corset, and underdrawers.

"I don't want to wear any of that," Maggie insisted. "It's the middle of August. I don't need stockings and I most certainly do not want a corset."

"No corset?!" Nora exclaimed. "What's going to hold you together?"

Nora's horrified expression made Maggie burst out with laughter. "Same as what holds you together, I imagine. My bones and skin. At least I hope so!" Sifting through the clothes hanging in her armoire, Maggie contemplated her Parisian purchases. "Here, look at this, Nora." She held up a straight-lined floral sheath of a translucent fabric, lined with green satin. It was worn with a coordinating billowy green tunic-length jacket. "Isn't it beautiful?"

"It's something, all right," Nora allowed. "You'll

certainly make an impression at the breakfast table. But wear it at your own risk. And don't be saying I selected it for you."

"I'll take the blame," Maggie agreed. Nora helped her change into the outfit. Truthfully, wearing something daring made her feel like her old self again. It felt good. "I'm starving. I take it I haven't missed breakfast?"

Pulling down her quick updo, Maggie shook her hair out, letting it spill around her shoulders, and began to brush. Without comment, Nora plucked the brush from her hand and continued the job. "No, you're in luck. His lordship's talk has delayed everything this morning."

"What on Earth is he babbling about for so long?"

"It's about those houseguests coming to live here at Wentworth Hall."

Maggie addressed Nora's face in the mirror. "Houseguests?" she asked. "Coming here? Whoever could they be? And how long will they be staying?"

"The Fitzhughs. Don't know more than that," Nora mumbled, holding a couple of pins in her mouth as she arranged Maggie's hair. "There," she said, admiring her handiwork.

Nora went off to take care of Lila, and Maggie headed down the hall. From the curved central staircase she could see the immense lobby below on the main floor of the estate. Most of the indoor staff of about thirty was assembled and listening to Lord Darlington's address. Craning over the balcony to hear his words, they came to her in a low drone. The staff could see her, though they dared not give any indication of it, but Lord Darlington's back was to Maggie and so he continued undisturbed.

Her father was dressed in a navy blue, single-breasted waistcoat, vest, and pants. His crisp white wing-collared shirt was nestled beneath a perfectly done black bow tie. His black shoes were polished daily and gleaming. As she descended the stairs, Maggie noted that the ever-widening bald spot on his head also held a shine and it amused her to imagine his manservant, Gerald, polishing it. Maggie would not put it beneath her father to request such a service.

"Are there any questions about what I have just said?" Lord Darlington asked the staff as Maggie settled on the stairs behind him.

"None at all, sir," Percival the head butler spoke for the others, standing with his usual square-shouldered perfect posture. "The young Fitzhughs shall be cared for with no less diligence than if they were His Royal Highness King Edward himself. We look forward to attending to their every need no matter how major or how minor. You can count on us, sir."

"I will count on it," Lord Darlington replied. "Indeed, I will insist upon it. You may dismiss the staff."

"Thank you, sir," Perceval said with a sharp nod.

Lord Darlington turned and noticed Maggie on the steps. "The Fitz-whos?" she asked.

"Maggie. Good to see you up and about this fine morning. I take it your travel malaise has lifted?" Lord Darlington held out his hand and helped Maggie up from the stairs. "And what, may I ask, are you wearing?" he asked, taking in her rather eccentric outfit as she stood up.

"It's the latest thing from Paris. Isn't it delightful? It's Aunt Daphne–approved."

Lord Darlington's face was less delighted. "Well, I'm not certain I approve. Though I am glad to see you, regardless of your attire. You will not wear that in England—and certainly not while we have houseguests."

"All right, Father. I will change if you insist. But first you must tell me, who are the Fitzhughs? And why are we hosting them with such fanfare?"

"You may have heard me speak of my days serving in the army during the Second Boer War in South Africa."

Endlessly, Maggie thought, and hoped she hadn't inadvertently rolled her eyes, a gesture her father deplored.

"Reginald Fitzhugh was my closest friend and during a particularly violent skirmish, he saved my life. Ever since then we have been closer than brothers."

"Then why have I never met him?" Maggie asked.

"Reggie went on to make his fortune in diamond trading, which required him to stay close to the diamond mines of South Africa," Lord Darlington explained. "We have corresponded avidly for the last twenty-five years."

"And now he's dead?"

"Sadly, yes. His wife also passed on many years before, and that leaves his children with no one to care for them but us."

"Us?" Maggie asked, the pitch of her voice rising, aghast at the thought of taking on any responsibility for small children. "How old *are* the little tykes?"

Abby Grahame

"You needn't worry, Maggie; Teddy and Jessica Fitzhugh are almost your age. They will both turn eighteen in a matter of months."

"They're twins?"

"Quite so, and given this tragic turn of events, they are dependent on our kindness. I expect you will treat them with the same warmth and hospitality as members of our family receive."

Members of our family receive about as much warmth as a snowstorm, Maggie considered, but decided not to voice her thoughts. "I'm sorry to hear of their father's death. But certainly, they must be perfectly capable of living on their own at their age?" she asked instead.

"Their fortune is being held in trust until they turn eighteen," Lord Darlington answered. "Their father made the contract iron-clad, I'm afraid. No way to get them any money a day before their birthdays."

"Ahh," Maggie said, amused that the plot had just thickened. It certainly explained her father's sudden and uncharacteristic benevolence.

"And what, might I ask, is meant by *ahh?*" Lord Darlington asked.

"Oh, nothing," Maggie replied with a cagey smile. He *knew* what she meant. The Darlington fortune was not what it once had been. The trappings were still there: the immense grandeur of Wentworth Hall, the staff of servants, the expensive clothing. But Maggie wasn't blind . . . or deaf . . . or dumb . . . and you would have to be all three to live in Wentworth Hall and not see that the family funds had been overspent and badly invested. A fresh infusion of a South African diamond fortune would be just the boost they needed. She wondered how her father planned to get his hands on the Fitzhugh fortune. Perhaps Wesley would have to return from Oxford and wed Miss Diamond Mines? She only hoped Jessica Fitzhugh was passably attractive, for her elder brother's sake.

The clatter of dishes being laid out could be heard from the dining room, and Maggie's stomach rumbled with hunger. She headed in the direction of the sound, but Lord Darlington clasped her at the elbow, halting her progress. "Upstairs, young lady, and change out of that Parisian getup."

Casting a longing eye toward the dining room, Maggie turned back and said, "Yes, Father." She started toward the staircase and began to climb.

Abby Grahame

"Maggie," Lord Darlington said, walking toward her, his expression turning thoughtful. "You have indeed become a most lovely young woman. There was a time, not long ago, when I worried about your . . . impulsive nature."

Stopping on the staircase, Maggie turned warily.

"It seems to me that your sojourn on the continent has lent you a new maturity that becomes you," he observed.

Maggie descended two steps, her heart sinking with this observation. By all accounts, her father's words were meant as a compliment. So why did it feel so insulting? Especially given the fact that he was right. Any spark of the girl she once was had been extinguished. She'd put it out herself.

"We should think about getting you out into society more. It's time we turned our attention to providing you with a suitable husband."

"Of course," Maggie snapped. "And I suppose you think Teddy Fitzhugh would be suitable?" she said, tossing off the words with worldly knowingness, making it clear that he was right to think her changed. She was no longer the wild unruly colt who had departed for the continent last year. She knew now how these games were played, and she was willing to play them.

"Perhaps," Lord Darlington replied in a level tone, "if he will have you. We also have more local suitors. Your mother would like to keep you close by, if possible. And the Duke of Cotswall has expressed interest." With that shocking revelation, he nodded his dismissal, turning his back and walking into his study.

Maggie gripped the curved banister to steady herself. Stunned by his words, she sank onto the step. This announcement had taken her utterly by surprise. It was the last thing she would have expected—or welcomed.

Chapter Two

"EXACTLY WHAT THIS FAMILY DOES *NOT* need," Nora complained. She trudged into the kitchen, arms piled high with dresses requiring laundering and pressing. Once more, Nora thought to herself how odd it was to come from upstairs where the Darlington family was slowly waking to face the day. Downstairs, the staff had been awake already for hours, preparing the morning meal and beginning their daily duties. They cleaned out the ashes from the fireplaces and lit new fires so the house would be warm when the family woke. Breakfast was already working. There were pots bubbling over with fragrant meals, breads baking in the oven, the sizzle of bacon in a fry pan. The dishes from the staff's breakfast earlier that morning were stacked in the sink. The cook's assistant would see to those once the Darlingtons had been fed. And all this for a highborn family of six! Well, five, with Lord Wesley away at Oxford. Nora shook her head again, muttering, "The Darlingtons have enough expenses without taking in orphans."

"And penniless orphans at that," replied Mrs. Howard. As the head housekeeper, Mrs. Howard was put in charge of keeping Wentworth Hall running. A difficult task, by any measure, and Mrs. Howard often looked pinched about the face, as if constantly in pain. It was hardly a secret that the family's ledgers were stretched to the limit. Not a day passed when Lord Darlington wasn't chastising his wife over some little luxury she'd bought the girls or a new piece of furniture she'd purchased for the baby's nursery. He'd always been an old cheapskate but these days more so than Nora could ever recall before.

Rose the cook looked up from pie dough she was patting into a dish. Something scrumptious she would serve the Darlingtons for lunch. "Oh, the Fitzhugh twins are far from penniless, I can assure you."

Mrs. Howard took a seat at the large round table in

the center of the room, pencil and pad in hand to begin creating a shopping list to stock the pantry in preparation for their guests. Nora stood beside her, sorting the clothes into piles on a chair.

"How do you know?" Mrs. Howard asked Rose. Nora was interested herself. It was rare for old Rose to have any gossip, confined to the kitchen as she was.

"The Fitzhughs have a summer estate in Kent and my sister's best friend is head housekeeper there. The staff dreads the months of June through August when the family returns from Johannesburg. Those twins are holy terrors and spoiled brats, to hear tell of it," Rose informed them. "Their summer estate can't keep a staff in place. They end up leaving the service after one season! That's why they aren't coming with their own valet and maid."

Helen, a young, plump housemaid with strawberry blond hair, emptied a bucket of gray water into the work sink. "I'm sure the poor things won't be as terrible as all that," she said as she wiped the bucket clean. "They are orphans now and have lost everything."

"It's true that they've lost their father and their mother

before that, but they haven't lost everything," Rose insisted. "In fact they stand to gain a great deal very soon, so I can't believe they will be with us for long."

"Mark my words, Lord Darlington will let them stay for as many months or years as they like," Mrs. Howard said. "As long as these two are heirs to a fortune, he'll treat them like gold. If only they would contribute to the household budget while they are here. Stretching the expenses to feed two more mouths is going to take a miracle, at this rate."

Nora handed the dresses over to Helen, with instructions from Lady Darlington to be more careful when ironing the lace this time. "Do you think they'll expect me to attend to Jessica Fitzhugh?" Nora asked, tucking her hair back into her white bonnet. "I certainly hope not," she added before anyone had a chance to answer. "My hands are completely full as it is, seeing to both Miss Maggie and Miss Lila. If this were a proper estate as it once was when my mother worked here, we would have twice the staff and be getting at least half again the twenty pounds a year we're earning."

"Oh, I don't know about that," Mrs. Howard disagreed.

"I have it for a fact that at the Duke's residence, Cotswall Manor, that's the case," Nora replied.

Abby Grahame

"Oh, Nora, you hear everything," Helen said with amusement, shaking her head as she sorted through the dresses Nora had presented to her.

"I do," Nora agreed. "It doesn't hurt to be informed." Nora made it a point to speak to others in service when she went into the town for the afternoon. And one of the great advantages of being a ladies maid was overhearing all sorts of information. Sometimes Lady Darlington acted as if Nora wasn't even there when she was talking to the girls.

"Oh, it's one thing to be informed, and another to be riling people up by spreading gossip," Grace, one of the upstairs maids, chided sourly as she wrung out a rag in the sink.

Nora glared at Grace for the implication. Grace loved to act like a know-it-all, which was rich, given the fact that she really knew nothing!

A tall, broad-shouldered young man with wavy black hair walked in the side entrance from the stables. Clear green eyes were the most striking feature of his square-jawed face. "Yes, tell us, Nora. What's the latest scandalous gossip?" He winked, a smile dancing on his lips.

Nora's hands went to her hips and she scowled at the handsome nineteen-year-old groom. Like her, Michael's father had worked at Wentworth Hall before him and he had grown up playing in the estate's immaculate many-stalled stable. While Nora had been orphaned at a young age, Michael still had his father, who tended Wentworth Hall's gardens. Knowing she was alone, Michael took special care of Nora. He was practically an older brother to her. Including the playful teasing.

"Oh, right, Michael, make fun now," she came back at him, "but when you want to know what's really going on around here, who do you go to? Me! That's who."

"And what would I want to know about this place?" he asked, pouring himself a glass of water from the cook's sink.

Nora tossed her head back and laughed. "Lots! You're more interested in the comings and goings than any of us maids."

"Hardly," Michael replied.

Nora guffawed. How many times had she reported to him on the whereabouts of one Lady Margaret Darlington? In that, he was always keenly interested.

Michael gave Nora a pointed look, and his dark brows knit as his green eyes thundered a warning for her not to say any more.

Nora shrugged her shoulders. Never let it be said that she didn't know the difference between sharing information and spreading rumors. There was plenty of scandal in Wentworth Hall that didn't get remarked upon. She had no intention of embarrassing Michael in front of everyone, but she couldn't resist the tease. "Well, I'm just saying is that each one of you has benefited one time or another from my *information*. So don't be so high and mighty about it," she scolded, wagging her finger at him.

Michael dropped comically to one knee in front of Nora and took her hand in a mock display of remorse. "I do humbly apologize, Nora."

"Ahh, get away from me," Nora rebuked him with a laugh. "You reek of horses. If I go upstairs smelling like that I'll hear about it from her ladyship and the girls."

"Maggie doesn't mind the smell of horses," Michael said, standing up.

"Has *Lady Margaret* been riding since she came home?" Mrs. Howard asked, emphasizing her proper title to make known her disapproval of the familiarity with which Michael and Nora often addressed Maggie and Lila.

"No . . . not yet, at any rate," Michael said. He turned

to refill his glass of water, and stood with his back to the room to look out the window.

"That's strange, don't you think, Michael?" Rose said as she laid apples and raisins into her pie. "Nearly a month since she returned and she hasn't even gone out to the stables? That girl always adored riding."

"Yes, she did," Michael agreed, then cleared his throat. "People change, I suppose."

Nora heard the sadness in his tone, and her heart went out to him. Michael had been living for the day when Maggie would return from her travels but since she'd come back, the girl hadn't as much as said hello to him.

"Lady Margaret *has* changed since she went to Europe," Mrs. Howard observed. "She's just not the happy wild thing she used to be. Have you noticed it, Michael? How does she seem to you?"

"I wouldn't know. I haven't set eyes on her," Michael admitted.

Nora moved to stand by him and realized he was hiding so they wouldn't see the red that had come to his cheeks at the mention of Maggie's name.

Nora caught his hand and gave it a squeeze, casting a sympathetic glance his way.

"The trip abroad has matured Lady Margaret," Grace ventured. "That's what an excursion like that is intended to do. Of course no one expected them to be gone as long as they were. Once Lady Darlington realized she was with child, I suppose they had no choice but to stay until the baby was born and hale enough to travel home. Now that they are back, I hear Lord and Lady Darlington are anxious to get Lady Margaret settled down, raising children of her own. And the Duke of Cotswall has been by Wentworth Hall a few times. . . ."

Nora looked sharply at the dowdy woman. Of course that was information Nora had already overheard, but she had been hoping to reveal it to Michael privately. Nora knew he had never stopped loving her—even knowing he was just a groom to her, and not someone Maggie could ever return feelings for. With darting eyes, Nora took in Michael's reaction. He had blanched white as one of the estate's crisp, starched sheets. "How do you know that?" Nora challenged Helen with a bit more aggression than she had meant to. "I never heard anything like that."

"I was mopping the hall the other day outside the library. The door was slightly open and I overheard the two of them talking," Grace explained.

"That's disgusting," Helen stated firmly, her voice dripping with true revulsion.

"What? That I overheard them?" Grace questioned. "It wasn't as though I was trying to—"

"No!" Helen interrupted. "The Duke of Cotswall marrying Lady Margaret—"

"I think he's rather distinguished," Mrs. Howard maintained. "For a man his age, I think—"

"That's exactly the thing of it," Helen insisted. "He's a man his age."

"What would you estimate him to be?" Rose asked Mrs. Howard. "Forty-five? Fifty?"

"It's not so unheard of," Mrs. Howard said. "A man of great wealth feels that the lavish life he can offer a young woman makes him an attractive candidate for marriage despite a gap in age, and many a young woman eagerly reciprocates his attentions."

"I still say it seems wrong," Helen said.

"That's because you're very young," Mrs. Howard replied.

Abby Grahame

"The opportunity to be the Duchess of Cotswall with all the power, influence, and opportunity which accompany that title is nothing to be dismissed lightly. I hope that the new sophistication and maturity that we are noticing in Lady Margaret will help her to realize what she's being offered."

"Disgusting," Helen mumbled, unimpressed, and walked off with an armful of dresses.

Michael had turned to face the room, listening to the conversation without joining in, standing deep in thought.

Looking to him, Mrs. Howard inquired, "What do you think of all this then, Michael? Of the duke?"

Michael said nothing at first. No emotion crossed his features. Then he simply said, "I think he's old."

Mrs. Howard lifted her eyebrow. "That's your only opinion? Don't you interact with him when he comes in his carriage?"

"He treats his horses well," Michael said dispassionately. "I haven't got much to judge him by, since he's not one to make conversation with a groom."

"I'm just surprised her ladyship is permitting the match," said Grace.

"Oh, nothing is set in stone yet," Nora put in. "And Lady

Maggie's not one to let anyone tell her what to do. I don't care how much she's changed, she would never take a husband she didn't care for. She's too much a romantic for that."

"I've got to get back to the horses," Michael said, abruptly placing his glass in the sink and hurrying out. The back door slammed behind him.

"What's gotten into him?" Mrs. Howard asked.

"Oh, you know he's concerned for his position," Rose pointed out. "A full stable with a groom is an expense Wentworth Hall might not be able to afford much longer. Especially now that no one goes riding. Why keep Michael on staff when they can simply employ Lord Darlington's valet to care for a couple horses instead?"

"Poor dear," Mrs. Howard said.

Therese descended the staircase, *"Bonjour,"* she greeted them shyly. She crossed to the pantry and took out the box of Nestle infant formula brought over from France especially for baby James. "May I heat this on the stove?"

"Allow me," Rose offered, taking the box and depositing its contents in a small pot she filled with water. "I really can't believe her ladyship has chosen not to breastfeed. Or even to get a wet nurse! This powder stuff is unnatural in my mind."

"Well, it serves its purpose," Therese demurred. Nora noticed Therese always had a diplomatic response to any bit of complaint or insult. "I just feel so badly for Lord James. The tiniest white teeth are popping through his gums already. The poor thing is in great pain."

"I'll put some hard bread on ice for the little dear," Rose said. "It will soothe him."

It took only minutes to warm the formula and deposit it in a baby bottle, also imported from the continent. "Merci," Therese said, before turning to hurry back up the stairs.

"Now there's the girl Michael should set his sights on," Rose commented. "So pretty and sweet."

"That she is," Mrs. Howard remarked pensively. "And familiar, somehow. Her smile . . . I feel like I've seen it before."

"I don't see how you could have," Rose said. "Unless you took a holiday to France on your afternoon off?"

"Very funny," Mrs. Howard replied. "I'm sure it's nothing. Her smile just reminds me of someone and I can't recall who."

"Déjà vu!" explained Grace.

"Excuse me?" Mrs. Howard asked, arching one eyebrow as though Helen had said something a bit racy.

"The French have a word for it," Grace explained. "It means you've seen something before in some other time and place; maybe even another lifetime."

"Oh, rubbish!" Mrs. Howard scoffed.

"Well, I say she's a lovely girl," Rose insisted.

"Do you think so?" Nora questioned skeptically.

"Don't you like her?" Rose asked.

"I'm not sure," Nora admitted. "There's something about her. We've been sharing quarters for weeks, and I barely know the first thing about her. She certainly keeps to herself."

"You're just annoyed you haven't gotten any gossip from her!" Grace taunted.

"The French *are* very different from us," Rose allowed. "More worldly, I think. It's a certain sophistication they seem to come by naturally."

"Maybe," Nora considered as she sat at the table. She couldn't imagine Michael with Therese, that much she knew. Although it did surprise her that Therese showed no interest in her handsome friend. Nora could practically hear the girls in town sigh whenever Michael walked by. In fact, Therese seemed preoccupied most of the time. Maybe she'd left behind a beau in France. Perhaps Nora could coax the story out of

Therese one day. The local newspaper, *The Sussex Courier*, lay in front of Nora and she began turning the pages, knowing she'd find juicy tidbits of local news in the society pages.

"Nora!" Mrs. Howard said sharply. "Why are you sitting there? Don't you have work to do?"

"Yes, ma'am." Her ladyship wouldn't want to dress for lunch for another half hour, so she actually did have some time to spare, but it never paid to appear idle in front of Mrs. Howard. If Nora had nothing to do, Mrs. Howard would find something. There was always a floor to be mopped or priceless heirloom to be dusted somewhere in the many, many hallways of the immense estate. "I'm going," Nora confirmed, tucking the newspaper into her apron pocket to be read in a less conspicuous spot.

As she climbed the servants' stairs, Nora heard Mrs. Howard speak to Rose. "I wish that girl were as committed to her work as she is to knowing everything that goes on around here," Mrs. Howard remarked.

"The girl is obsessed with snooping," Grace added.

Rose laughed warmly in agreement. "She is a regular busybody, isn't she?"

Turning, Nora wrinkled her nose at them disagreeably.

Chapter Three

The Sussex Courier

Introducing:
MISFORTUNE MANOR!

The well-heeled denizens of the local mansions, estates, halls, and other of the area's palatial dwellings are all atwitter. What has set these regal folks talking? It is nothing less unexpected that the sudden appearance of that most maligned yet coveted phenomenon known as "New Money." How dreadful . . . yet thrilling. How they disdain it! How they want it!

These youthful visitors with dizzying wealth may have come from a land overseas where jungle animals hunt their prey . . . but they will be surprised to find that in the land of impoverished gentry, they are the prey! Hunted by Lords and Ladies wielding their poor but titled unmarried sons and daughters, trying to ensnare the moneyed youth in the marriage trap.

Not even England's oldest and most well respected family is beyond this behavior. In fact, they might be the most desperate of all. . . .

Stay tuned, dear readers, for the first thrilling installment of MISFORTUNE MANOR . . . coming next week!

Chapter Four

"No!" LILA CRIED AS NORA BEGAN TO pull Lila's dark blond hair back into its usual French braid. "I don't want my hair like this today, Nora." She gazed imploringly at Nora's reflection in the mirror. "Can't we do it differently?"

Nora scowled, confused. "Did you have something special in mind?" she asked.

Lila sighed, feeling just slightly foolish. This morning the Fitzhugh twins would arrive and she wanted to make the right first impression. It was bad enough that Maggie treated her as though she were a child, even though there was a mere two years' difference in their ages. Lila didn't want Jessica and Teddy Fitzhugh also thinking she was a little girl to be ignored. She had missed the excitement of Paris, and Lila was determined not to be shut out of this new excitement.

"You could try a twist in back," Lila suggested to Nora.

"A French twist!" Nora cried, aghast at the idea. "Your mother would never allow it. Girls of sixteen don't wear their hair like that."

"Seventeen in two months," Lila objected with a pout.

"What if I tie it at the nape of your neck with a blue ribbon?" Nora said. "It's not quite as girlish as a braid."

Lila considered this alternative before nodding her consent. "That would be better, I suppose," she allowed.

When Nora had finished brushing and tying the ponytail in place, Lila stood in front of her dressing room mirror. The white linen dropped waist frock she wore completely obliterated any sign of her developing curves. She tugged at the collar so at least a bit of collarbone was revealed. "Hopeless," she murmured.

"Oh, I wouldn't fret," Nora said consolingly. "I'm sure the Fitzhugh twins will like you as much as we all do."

"And pay about as much attention to me as everyone around here does, also," Lila sulked. "It's as though I'm neither fish nor foul—not a child and not an adult. Sometimes I feel like a ghost—invisible and completely—"

Lila cut herself short as the sound of a motorcar approached, its engine growing ever noisier on the road in front of the manor. "It's them!" Lila shouted, rushing to the window. Pushing aside the curtain, she peered down at the gleaming red vehicle. Its open top revealed a young man and woman in the front seat. The woman in the front passenger seat wore a fur-trimmed knit sweater. Her sleek finger-curls were swept back in a twisting chignon that elegantly spanned the nape of her neck. Jeweled bracelets were piled up both arms.

But Lila's eyes were glued on the driver.

Auburn-haired and athletically built, he reeked confidence. It was in his squared shoulders and the regal upward tilt of his chiseled jaw. He wore a white cable-knit sweater under a blue blazer. "Oh, look at him, Nora!" Lila gushed. "Isn't Teddy Fitzhugh gorgeous?!"

"Quite the modern man," Nora agreed with a sour note in her voice that caught Lila by surprise.

She turned to face her maid. "What does that mean?"

"Not a thing," Nora insisted, gathering the nightgown Lila had allowed to drop to the floor.

"It means something," Lila insisted.

"I like to reserve my judgments until I meet a person."

"Oh, he's going to be wonderful, Nora!" Lila said assuredly. "I can tell just by looking at him." Lila bounded toward the door. "Why am I standing here? I have to greet them."

Lila heard Nora say something about Percival the butler admitting them as she rushed into the hall. Her mother and Maggie were already ahead of her, both deep in conversation. Lila fell back, not wanting to join them, her enthusiasm deflated by the fact that her sister looked spectacular in a silk floral dress that followed her womanly figure, not exactly hugging her body but certainly accentuating its form. Her abundant hair was gathered in a loose knot at the top of her head. A vision of effortless elegance.

How could she ever compete with that?

Teddy Fitzhugh would be swept off his feet—just like every other young man Maggie deigned to look upon.

But maybe not! This was a fresh start with new people. Lila resolved to assert herself, make her presence known.

Picking up her pace, Lila caught up to her mother and sister. "Isn't it exciting?" she said.

Her mother glanced over her shoulder and nodded. Maggie, as usual, didn't even acknowledge Lila's presence.

"It is indeed," Lady Darlington agreed. "I was just telling your sister that she should make every effort to get to know Teddy Fitzhugh. She's ready for marriage and the longer she waits the dimmer her prospects will become."

"Marriage?" Lila gasped. Teddy Fitzhugh wasn't even in the door yet and they were already plotting to marry him to Maggie. "Surely you can't be serious."

"Have no doubt, I am most serious," Lady Darlington said.

"I saw him from my window. He's not terrible-looking," Maggie said, her voice flat with the new, put-on maturity she'd acquired over the last year. It was so affected it made Lila want to scream. Only one year earlier they'd tickled, poked, and teased each other, racing down the halls of the manor laughing like lunatics. But now, since her return, Lila hardly recognized her sister. It was as if Maggie had had her heart surgically removed while in France. The change in Maggie was mystifying and depressing—and insufferable.

"I'd say he was rather handsome," Lila grumbled.

Maggie shrugged as if already bored.

Lila fought the urge to choke her sister as they hurried down the staircase. At the bottom of the stairs, Percival was admitting the twins. "Welcome! Welcome!" Lady Darlington exclaimed, hurrying into the foyer, her arms outstretched in an embracing gesture of charm and warmth. "Welcome to Wentworth Hall. We're so delighted you're both here."

Teddy Fitzhugh reached back and lifted something from atop one of his suitcases. Turning forward, he offered Lady Darlington a lavishly abundant bouquet of mixed-color roses. "We are so grateful for your kindness to us, Lady Darlington," he said as he presented them.

"Most grateful," Jessica Fitzhugh echoed with less sincere warmth than her brother.

Lila hoped her face didn't reveal how overwhelmed she felt by the mere sight of Teddy. She had never seen any man like him. For one thing, he was tan. Set against his sun-lightened hair and eyes it spoke to her of outdoor adventure and highlighted his pearly teeth in a way that gave his smile a thrillingly dangerous charm.

"Thank you. They're exquisite," Lady Darlington gushed over the roses.

Lila opened her mouth to agree with her mother but closed it again when Lady Darlington added, "Aren't they stunning, Maggie?"

"Beautiful," Maggie concurred without much enthusiasm.

"Yes, beautiful," Teddy Fitzhugh murmured. Lila followed the direction of his gaze and immediately realized it was fixed on Maggie. It was as if he could see nothing else.

For Lila, it was a kick in the gut.

It took only two days for Lila to conclude that there was absolutely no hope of distracting Teddy Fitzhugh from his fascination with Maggie. Teddy was polite to Lila, of course. During dinner he responded to her questions about South Africa. He encouraged her to play the piano for them at tea. But Lila knew this attention was out of courtesy, not genuine interest. When Lila's older sister was in the room he did nothing but hang on her every word, laughing uproariously at her every pale witticism, scowling with concern whenever she voiced the mildest of complaints. To borrow an expression she'd heard Nora use: He was hooked. There was nothing Lila could think of that could possibly make him notice her. Unless, of course, she had an ally.

It couldn't be just any ally, either. It had to be someone who knew him well and whom he trusted completely. Lila came up with a plan.

Jessica Fitzhugh was, in her own way, as strikingly attractive as her brother. She too had the light tan her brother sported, laid over with a spray of freckles across her high cheekbones and delicate nose. With her fashionable finger-curls and chignon combined with a graceful yet athletic gait, Jessica Fitzhugh seemed to Lila to be the height of modern womanhood. And as such, Lila found the more sophisticated and somewhat older Jessica to be utterly intimidating and dauntingly unapproachable. It didn't help matters that Jessica mostly kept to herself. Lila thought she must be homesick and also missing her father terribly. Nora confided that she thought Jessica was simply a snob—pointing to Jessica's constant sour expression as proof. But Lila didn't want to believe it. Maybe that was just how Jessica's face looked in repose. She couldn't help that.

But if Lila could befriend Jessica she would have the inside track on Teddy. She'd never seen a brother and sister who were closer, probably because they were also twins. Besides that, it would be nice to have a friend at Wentworth Hall, someone to fill the void Maggie had left since deciding she was too grown-up to bother with Lila any longer.

There didn't seem any way into Jessica's world, though. She spent all her time with Teddy and if he was off trailing after Maggie, she busied herself in her room either reading or scribbling in a red notebook she seemed to carry with her everywhere. But one afternoon Lila came upon Jessica studying the oil portraits that lined the upstairs hallway.

"That's my brother Wesley," Lila said, sidling up beside Jessica, who was standing below the portrait of the oldest Darlington sibling and gazing up at it.

"Really," Jessica remarked without turning toward Lila but continuing to inspect the painting.

"I call him Wes, for short. He studies at Oxford University, though right now he's in the states with a school chum. I miss him terribly. He dotes on me. We're very close, just like you and Teddy."

Abby Grahame

Jessica turned to look at Lila, her face twisted into a disdainful smile. "I doubt it."

Lila hadn't been prepared for such a condescending response. "What do you doubt?" she asked, surprised.

"That your relationship resembles my bond with Teddy in any way. We're twins."

"Well, of course," Lila agreed, feeling horribly foolish and hoping her face wasn't turning red. "I suppose one can't ever understand what it's like to be a twin unless one is, oneself, a twin."

"Exactly," Jessica said, returning her gaze to the portrait of Wesley. "I must say he's not bad-looking."

"Who, Wes? Oh, no, Wes is very handsome. All the girls think so."

"How do you know? Do they confide in you?" Jessica scoffed.

"Sometimes," Lila insisted, her voice rising a bit. This was not going as planned. Why was Jessica being so disagreeable? She hoped Jessica wouldn't press her for an instance of this happening because she couldn't think of one. Even if no girl had ever actually told Lila she admired Wes, Lila could tell that girls liked her older brother. It was obvious from the coy and giggly way they acted in his presence. "You can see from his portrait that he's handsome, can't you?" Lila added. What more proof did she need?

"Hmmm," Jessica hummed as she considered the question, her chin still tilted up to Wesley's image.

Lila couldn't believe that the question of Wes's good looks required this much consideration. "What about him disturbs you?" she challenged, instantly regretting the touch of peevishness that had crept into her tone.

"No . . . no . . . you're right. In this portrait he's very handsome, but portrait painters make their commissions by flattering their subjects, don't they?"

"I assure you, this is what he looks like," Lila maintained.

"Take the case of the portrait of your mother hanging over the fireplace in the living room for instance," Jessica countered. "She doesn't really look like that now, does she? I mean, there's absolutely no sign of that double chin of hers and she's quite a bit more svelte than in real life."

"What do you mean by a double chin?"

Jessica patted the underside of her own chin. "That."

Lila had never paid attention to it before, but now that

she pictured Lady Darlington she realized that her mother did have a soft pad of fat under her chin. "Well, that painting was done right after my parents were married, so it must be at least twenty years old. I think she was nineteen when they married."

"So that's my point," Jessica stated firmly. "How do I know that handsome Wes here hasn't grown chubby on university beer and pub food while he's been off supposedly studying? Maybe that pale blond hair has even begun to recede. Some men begin balding as early as their twenties, you know."

Lila found this idea not only horrifying but insulting. "I'm sure that Wes has not grown fat and bald in the less than a year since I last saw him."

Jessica shrugged noncommittally. "I'm simply saying that what one sees in a painting is not always what one gets. Wentworth Hall, for instance. Before Teddy and I agreed to come stay here, your father sent our solicitor who minds our affairs a small painting of the place. It appeared quite elegant."

"Don't you think it is elegant?"

"It's probably not so different than in your mother's

case," Jessica replied with a sneering grin as she began strolling off down the hallway away from Lila.

"I don't understand," Lila admitted.

"It's seen better days," Jessica shot back from over her shoulder, clearly delighted with her quip.

Lila fumed, watching Jessica's back swing lightly back and forth as she sauntered down the hall looking insufferably pleased with herself. Why would someone take such glee in being insulting? What had Lila—indeed, any of the Darlingtons—ever done to Jessica other than try to be nice? Was it worth Lila's effort to even attempt being friendly in the future?

It baffled Lila to think that Jessica and Teddy could be twins. Surely they were not a thing alike. But then, she and Maggie were sisters, close in age, and Lila was certain that she did not in any way resemble her heartless, stuck-up sister. And, hopefully, Teddy would come to discover that before very long.

Chapter Five

YOUR HORSE, M'LADY," MICHAEL SAID.
He handed Maggie the reins of the bay mare
he'd saddled for her. Michael hoped she heard
the ironic formality in his tone. It wasn't so long ago that
Michael used to lift Maggie to her horse with his hands
on her waist. How far they'd grown. Teddy and Jessica
Fitzhugh stood waiting for their horses by the stable door
but they were engaged in polite conversation and he felt
confident that neither of them would notice the private
look that darted between the two of them. It was only a
flicker, because in a twinkling Maggie averted those fath-
omless brown eyes he adored.

"Look at me," he murmured urgently. "For God's sake!"
This was the first time he'd seen her since her return. Who

knew when he'd have the chance to be this close to her again? He had to know what had happened during her year away. What had changed her like this? Why had she grown so cold toward him? She hadn't even given him a chance to apologize. . . .

When Maggie returned her gaze to him, her eyes were blank slates, devoid not only of feeling but even recognition. "Thank you, Michael," she said in a neutral tone loud enough to be heard by everyone. "Thank you for remembering I like the D-ring bridle."

"Of course I know which—"

"Have you saddled the other three horses?" Maggie cut him off.

"Stop it, would you?" Michael implored, his tone low but becoming increasingly agitated. This made no sense. What was wrong with her?

Maggie's eyes bore into him now, shading into a stormy gray warning. Tilting her chin to gaze over his shoulder, she called to the Fitzhugh twins. "The groom will have your horses for you right away."

"The groom?" Michael echoed, his voice an angry rumble.

Abby Grahame

"That's what you are," Maggie said with a patrician nod, "or am I mistaken about that?"

Michael felt caught between the urges to shake her for her detached denigration or to sweep her in his arms to remind her of what had once been between them. Instead, he masked the hurt with a clipped civility. "As you wish, Lady Margaret," he said with just the merest bow and turned toward the stable.

Fuming, he led out two chestnut geldings for Jessica and Teddy Fitzhugh and then brought the delicate black Arabian mare he knew Lila favored. In minutes all four of them were mounted. "I heard you were quite the rider, Lady Margaret," Teddy said. "Now that I see you astride the horse I can see you are, indeed, a natural horsewoman."

"I used to be an avid rider," Maggie agreed. "But not as much of late."

"Will you come with us, Michael?" Lila invited him. "There's a trail that borders Cotswall Manor that I've been dying to try."

"Yes, it's an old trail, but the gardeners cleared the brush from it just a few weeks ago,"

"Oh, good, you know it, then," Lila enthused. "I

don't want to trespass on Cotswall property, though. Will you come and make sure we don't stray onto the duke's property?"

Michael hesitated, torn about whether or not to go with them. On the one hand he couldn't stand to see Maggie around that fawning Teddy Fitzhugh. Teddy was so clearly smitten with Maggie that it was almost comical. Though Michael could hardly blame Teddy. He knew too well how it felt to be under Maggie's spell. Still, Teddy irked him with his preening overconfidence and smug air of entitlement. On the other hand, if he accompanied them he might get another opportunity to speak to Maggie alone.

"Will you come?" Lila urged again.

"Lila, Michael has chores to do, I'm sure," Maggie chided her sister in a superior tone.

Michael's eyes darted between the sisters as he tried to understand what was really happening. Why was Lila so intent on his accompanying them?

"Look at Maggie on that horse, Jessica," Teddy spoke to his sister. "Doesn't she just look so right there? I've noticed that other English riders are rigid in the saddle, but not Maggie."

Michael glanced at Teddy, unable to disguise his dislike. The fawning fool! Preening fop! Couldn't he see that Maggie was only toying with him?

And then he saw it. It was written all over Lila's face. It was almost embarrassingly clear in the way she gazed at Teddy with nearly unabashed adoration. Lila hoped Maggie would be distracted with Michael joining them, giving her more opportunity to talk to Teddy. Michael would be happy to oblige. Maybe he could melt Maggie's frosty demeanor.

"Yes, I should come," Michael said. "The path is a bit difficult to follow up there and you might wander into Cotswall Manor by mistake."

"I'm sure the Duke of Cotswall wouldn't be too put out to see Maggie riding on his land," Lila said with a shrewd grin.

After what Michael had heard in the kitchen he understood what she was getting at. If Lila was trying to show Teddy that Maggie had other suitors, her plan was bound to backfire. It would only serve to make Teddy jealous. Michael was sure of that. He himself felt the jealousy rising within him.

"The Duke of Cotswall is old enough to be my grand-father," Maggie scoffed.

"Surely he's not much older than Father," Lila countered.

Maggie laughed. "Is that any better?"

"No better," Teddy put in emphatically.

"Isn't he terribly wealthy, though?" Jessica asked.

"Nora hears that he's positively loaded," Lila answered, using the exact slang Nora had.

"Lila!" Maggie scolded. "It doesn't matter to me how rich he is. I would never consider marrying the duke."

"Of course not!" Teddy agreed. "There are other men, younger men with just as much wealth who are sure to fall in love with you; a man you could have a real life with, not some antiquated codger."

Michael schooled his features to reveal no emotion, but inwardly glowered at Teddy. He was so sure of him-self, so confident that he was the one who would capture Maggie's heart, so certain that his wealth and shallow charm would make him the winner in the end.

Maggie sat forward in her saddle, signaling that she was eager to get going. "All this talk of marriage is giving me a headache," she announced. "I want to ride and forget about old dukes and wealthy young men. Let's go."

With a flick of her reins, and a sharp click to her horse, Maggie was off. Not wanting to be left behind, the others took off after her.

Michael shook his head woefully, watching them thunder across the lawn toward the wooded trail. Everyone was talking about how France had changed Maggie, but deep down she was the same, headstrong and determined to have her own way. She hadn't wanted Michael to join them and she'd found a way to leave before he could saddle up.

For a moment, Michael considered going after them, certain he could easily overtake them, but decided against it. No good could come of him being in the presence of that strutting Teddy Fitzhugh. Michael would eventually do or say something to make his feelings known, and he couldn't risk losing his job.

A knot constructed of anger, jealousy, and frustration twisted in his gut. By a mere accident of birth—his own low station in life—he was denied the person he loved most in the world. The woman he would always love and long for. The woman he believed loved him still, no matter how much she pretended not to.

* * *

"You have very delicate hands," Nora observed, speaking to Therese that night as they cleared their own dishes from the servants' table. As the last to finish eating, what was left of the cleanup had fallen to them. She'd noticed Therese's hands for the first time as the young woman lifted a platter that had been heaped with mutton chops and potatoes.

Therese spread her hands wide and observed them as if assessing their delicacy for the first time ever. "*Oui*, perhaps they are. My hands are strong, though."

Nora gazed at her own solid fingers and ragged nails and decided she should take better care of them. They certainly marked her as someone who worked hard for a living. "People judge you by your hands," she remarked, piling dishes in the sink.

"I will give you some of my hand cream. I need to have soft hands to work with the baby."

"That's very kind of you," Nora remarked in a tone that was a bit guarded. She hadn't yet made up her mind about Therese. "Is it French hand cream?"

"It is," Therese said, scraping the remaining food from

a plate into the garbage. "My mother always used it."

"Were you in service as a child?" Nora probed. "I've been in service since I was a child because my mother was employed here. When she died, the Darlingtons kept me on. I'd have been an orphan if they hadn't been kind to me in that way."

"It must have been lonely for you," Therese sympathized.

Nora shrugged. "I missed my mother, of course, but the rest of the staff were a kind of family. Maggie and Lila are like family to me."

Therese looked away and Nora couldn't read the expression that washed over her face. "What is it?" Nora asked.

"How can you have family who live such a completely different life from you? Didn't you resent that you were their servant? It's as though you were Cinderella and they were your wicked stepsisters."

Nora considered this for a moment before speaking. Did she resent Lila and Maggie? She didn't think it was fair, being born into privilege or poverty. But she didn't blame the girls for that. "It's just how it's always been," Nora explained.

"And that's all right with you?" Therese challenged.

"I have my plans for bettering myself," Nora insisted. "But it's not the Darlingtons' fault that my mother was a maid and my father was also a servant who died young. What were they supposed to do, share their wealth with us? That was not about to happen. And besides, if they hadn't given my parents jobs we'd have been poorer still."

Therese fell silent, pensive. Nora thought the line of conversation was odd, but perhaps this was also down to Therese's "Frenchness." The French were a philosophical bunch, after all.

When the kitchen was cleared and the table cleaned, Nora took out some of Lady Darlington's dresses that she'd laid aside to mend. Taking her sewing kit from a cabinet, she sat down at the table to attend to it before retiring for the night.

"I can help you with that," Therese offered. "Give me that one with the ripped lace collar. I'm good with lace. My mother taught me to tat."

Nora shifted the lace-collared dress over to Therese. "Tatting is lace making?"

Therese nodded. "My mother was also a maid but she

saved enough to open a flower shop eventually."

"That's very inspiring," Nora said sincerely. She loved stories of servants who had gotten out of the service and done well. It was what she wanted for herself.

"She was a maid for Lord Darlington's sister in France."

"The aunt they stayed with in Paris," Nora recalled.

"Yes. After my mother died and the shop closed I went back there to see if I could find some work to support myself. That's when I met Lady Maggie and her mother and they hired me to take care of the baby."

"That worked out well, then," Nora remarked as she began to stitch a dropped hem on a green taffeta gown.

"I'm not so sure," Therese commented.

"What do you mean? Don't you like it here?"

Therese shirked her slim shoulders in a gesture of ambivalence. "I mean no offense, but I find the English to be cold."

The right side of Nora's lip kicked up in a bemused grin. "You have to get to know us."

"Most of the staff has been kind but I find the Darlingtons to be snobbish, especially Lord Darlington, and his daughter Lady Maggie is also."

"Maggie didn't used to be," Nora said. "Something

changed her while she was away. She used to be a wild spitfire, always full of fun. I remember once when her family hosted a fox hunt. She felt so sorry for the fox that she led Michael, me, and Lila out to catch the fox before it had gone very far. We hid it and ourselves in the old abandoned caretaker's cottage. We were turning red from trying not to laugh when all the hounds were outside barking and no one could figure out why." Nora put down her work and laughed at the childhood memory. "Even though we helped, it was all Maggie's idea."

Therese smiled, amused by the story. "Good for you. I think fox hunting is barbaric."

Nora shook her head, still laughing. "What fun we had! Maggie was always the one coming up with the mischief and we were all for it."

Therese lifted her chin and listened attentively to some sound that had caught her attention. One of the many call bells that lined the wall near the doorway was jingling. "It's coming from the nursery," Therese realized, rising from her chair. "Little James must have awakened. I have to go."

"Good luck."

Therese crossed to the icebox and extracted one

of the frozen bagels Rose had prepared for the teething baby. "I'll return if he falls back to sleep quickly," she promised.

"Thanks," Nora said as Therese left.

Resuming her sewing, Nora assessed her new opinion of Therese. She'd changed since she first arrived, had become more friendly, more like one of the staff. Maybe she was simply starting to relax. Or had something happened to sour her on the Darlingtons? "Hmm," Nora hummed pensively. If Therese was having trouble with her position in the Darlington household, Nora would just have to get to the bottom of it.

Chapter Six

The Sussex Courier

MISFORTUNE MANOR!

The most coveted houseguests have arrived at Faded Glory Manor, and not a moment too soon!

The moneyed Sterling twins are in a bit of a pickle: Their mounds of cash are tied up due to their deceased father's strict rules on their inheritance. With three months until their eighteenth birthday, and no relatives to speak of, Richard and Richina Sterling have no choice but to hole up in Faded Glory Manor, home of their late father's wartime comrade, Lord Worthless.

But Faded Glory Manor is not quite the lap of luxury the Sterling twins have come to expect. The drafty old home once knew greatness, but can barely afford a maid for each lady of the house these days! Fallen on hard times, indeed.

The twins were in for a rude awakening the moment they arrive.

The entire staff was assembled inside to greet them, watching as Richie leapt over the side of the car, heels clicking together, and gold coins dropping from his pocket. He saw them but couldn't be bothered to pick them up as he hurried to open Richina's door. "It's definitely the right address. This is Faded Glory Manor,

Sister dear," he said. "It certainly has seen better days, but we've been invited to stay and it would be poor form not to, so let's make the best of it, shall we?"

Richina extended a hand dripping in diamond rings and bracelets. "If you insist."

"Don't worry," Richie assured her. "I'll have a tennis court installed over the weekend."

At the twenty-foot-high front door, Richie banged on the enormous brass knocker and the twins were instantly engulfed in a swirling dust storm. "It seems no one has been here for a while," Richie observed while Richina coughed spasmodically against the door. She was nearly toppled as, with a deafening creak, the door opened.

A skeleton in filthy butler attire greeted them. "We've been expecting you."

Exchanging a dubious and wary look, the twins followed him into the rotted and decaying hall, a spectacle of past glory in desperate need of upkeep. A sad-looking maid and seemingly senile valet stood in the hall. "This can't be the entire staff!" stage-whispered Richina to her equally horrified brother. Richina wiped the grime from her forehead, setting off another deafening clatter of jewelry.

A woman's voice trilled from the dayroom. "Diamonds? Do I hear diamonds?" The lady of the estate, Lady Worthless, stumbled out, intoxicated by the sound. "I once had diamonds. Where is that beautiful music coming from?"

"Do you mean these?" Richina asked and shimmied with arms outstretched, her many diamonds, bracelets, necklaces, and brooches creating such a commotion that a large chunk of plaster falls from the ceiling.

Alerted by the sound of the rattling diamonds, Lord Worthless walked in. Stepping over the hunk of fallen plaster, he shook Richie Sterling's hand. "How do you do?" he asked.

"We're not quite sure," Richie admitted, eyeing the plaster under the Lord's feet. "Do things like this often happen here?"

"Things like what?" Lord Worthless inquired.

"That plaster on the floor," Richie said, pointing.

"I say, I don't have the foggiest idea what you mean," Lord Worthless said, his expression vague. "Have you met my daughters yet?"

"I'm here, father." The twins heard the voice but saw no one.

"Stop fooling, Doodles, and show yourself," Lord Worthless demanded.

"But I'm right here," Doodles Worthless insisted.

Lord Worthless turned to his wife for help but she had become completely bedazzled by Richina's jewelry and could only stare at it, her eyes two saucers of yearning. He clapped his hands sharply. "Come off it!" he demanded. "Why can't we see Doodles?"

Lady Worthless roused from her dazed state. "Doodles? Oh, she must have blended in with the wallpaper again." She smiled apologetically at Richie and Richina as she walked over to the floral-patterned wall and reached in. Doodles Worthless suddenly emerged. "What have I told you about standing so close to the wall?" her mother scolded.

"Don't you have another daughter?" Richie recalled.

Lord Worthless turned to his wife. "Do we?"

Lady Worthless tittered with laugher. "Why, of course we do, you old fool. Our eldest daughter Snobby is around here somewhere." Lady Worthless suddenly eyed Richie with a new alertness as if an idea occurred to her. "You might like Snobby. She's going to make some lucky man a fine wife someday. She never lets her enthusiasms run wild, as some young women do. In fact, she has no enthusiasm for anything."

"Hmm," Richie demurred. "I don't know."

"Unless you'd prefer Doodles here," Lady Worthless suggested, searching around for her youngest daughter who has dropped out of sight once more. "Doodles?"

Abby Grahame

"Yes, Mother," Doodles's voice wafted in from the wallpapered wall.

"Oh, not again," Lady Worthless muttered. She headed over to retrieve her daughter but Richie stopped her.

"Never mind," he said. "I'm too young to marry just yet."

"Never too young when a fortune is at stake," Lady Worthless disagreed. "A good wife can help you spend—I mean *manage*—it. Yes, manage is what I meant to say . . . not spend . . . manage. Snobby will be a very sensible manager."

Snobby glided into the room. "Did someone mention my name?" she asked in her low, husky voice.

Lady Worthless smiled charmingly at Richie.

"Why, yes, dear, I was just telling—"

"Never mind," Snobby cut her mother off. "I've lost interest. My mind has drifted back to my days on the Continent where things were interesting, not like they are here in England. I'm never quite *here* because I'm always *there*."

"Hopefully my sister and I will liven things up around here," Richie suggested.

"I doubt it," Snobby replied with a yawn.

"You look familiar. Perhaps you run in the same circles as my sister here," Richie said.

Snobby cast him a disdainful glance. "I would never run in circles."

"I could show you my diamonds," Richina offered.

"Not interested," Snobby declines as she glides out of the room.

"I'd like to see them," Lady Worthless said excitedly, her eyes swirling once more as she went back into a diamond-envy–induced trance state.

"If you'll excuse me, I must go and count the family heirlooms," Lord Worthless said, checking the watch fob in his vest pocket. "I do it every day at this time." He headed for the nearest door, but the crystal doorknob came off in his hand. Dropping it, he wandered off in search of another way out.

Richie turned to his sister. "See, Sis? It's not so bad."

"No, it's worse!" Richina stated. She took Richie by the hand and headed out of the room, pulling him after her. "Come, Richie, dear. Let's go call a man about putting in that tennis court. At least if we play tennis we won't have to talk to these impecunious lunatics."

The room empted but a small voice could be heard from the wall. "Where is everyone going? Can I come?"

Poor Doodles. Is there anything worse than being forgotten?

And so dear reader, we hope your imaginations can supply the further comings and goings at Faded Glory Hall until the next thrilling installment of MISFORTUNE MANOR.

Abby Grahame

Chapter Seven

ILA DARLINGTON WAS STEWING. IT WAS NOT an unfamiliar feeling.

She'd tried going into the nursery to play with baby James, but Therese had told her he was asleep. Even baby James had better things to do than spend time with Lila. She was seated in the library, rereading *The Secret Garden* for what felt like the umpteenth time.

She closed her novel with a heavy sigh, and walked over to see what other reading options there might be on the shelves. Maybe a new volume had magically appeared in their collection. Not that Father was in the habit of book buying these days. The only new books they ever received were gifts from Wesley. The library looked out onto the considerable garden at Wentworth Hall, and movement on the grounds caught her attention. She pushed back the curtain and peered down. Her attention was fixed on the young man and woman strolling across it: Teddy Fitzhugh and Maggie.

He seemed to slow his walk to accommodate Maggie's graceful strides, laughing hilariously at her every droll remark. It was infuriating. And Lady Darlington encouraged them! Although it was odd to Lila that Mother was so focused on marrying off Maggie when Wes was the heir. Not that Teddy seemed to mind. He was hopelessly smitten with her older sister.

Who wasn't?

Ever since Lila could remember, boys vied for Maggie's attention. Whether at the country dances they were allowed to attend, or formal luncheons while they were in London, Maggie commanded an audience. Even Michael the stable groom had been mad for Maggie. And Maggie had given Michael plenty of opportunity to fall in love with her. Every second of the day she'd been down at the stable either saddling up to ride or grooming her own horses, Buckingham and Windsor. Her mother called Maggie "my equestrian" but Lila wasn't fooled. Maggie was there to see Michael. Before Maggie had left for France, Lila believed Maggie considered Michael a friend, that she was oblivious to his obvious real feelings for her. That she simply craved the attention.

And then abruptly, without warning, Maggie lost all interest in the horses, and Michael. As if they were toys she had grown tired of.

During their year apart, Lila had gone from hating Maggie for leaving her behind, to forgiving her once she realized Maggie was trapped in Southern France with their pregnant mother, back to hating her for never returning Lila's letters.

Lila had been willing to look past all of that in order to spend time with Maggie again. And now that Lila was just a year away from having her own season in London, she had all sorts of questions for Maggie about Parisian style and London's gentry. But these days, her elder sister simply avoided her. She wouldn't even talk about her time in France! It was positively selfish.

The last year had been so lonely! If only Wesley hadn't been gone too. The oldest Darlington had always doted on Lila, made her feel special. He'd taken her on hikes with him and taught her to play darts and throw horseshoes. He'd never looked down on her because she was younger or a girl. Because of him, she'd been something of a tomboy growing up, always eager to prove to him that she could keep up.

It was hard to believe, but Lila realized now that Maggie was back and the Fitzhughs were staying at Wentworth Hall, Lila felt more alone than ever. She missed Wes. Lila hoped he'd find some time to come visit before starting at Oxford again for the new fall semester.

Lila absently twirled her dark blond hair and walked back to her bedroom. Why did Maggie dazzle while Lila was always overlooked? Maybe she didn't have Maggie's quick wit, mischievous smile, and soft beauty, but Lila knew her angular features, blond curls, and brown eyes weren't *completely* without charm. And she was certainly the kinder of the two sisters (in Lila's opinion). It had to be her shy nature that made her so much less attractive than her older sister. It wasn't that she didn't want to assert herself around others. She did! But it was difficult to struggle against one's own natural temperament and be anything other than what she was.

"Fresh underclothes, washed and pressed." Nora

Abby Grahame

entered the bedroom behind Lila carrying a pile of white ruffled petticoats, camisoles, and knickers. "I got you a corset, too," Nora added with a conspiratorial wink. "Though, don't tell your mum, she doesn't think it's appropriate for a girl of sixteen. It used to be one of Maggie's, but she won't miss it. She hates the thing."

Lila snapped the white corset from the top of the pile and wrapped it around her waist. "Oh, Nora, you're an angel! Would you lace it up for me?"

"I'm not going to do it up over your jumper," Nora said with a laugh. "Take off your dress and we'll do it proper."

Lila tossed her jumper over her head, throwing the sailor-style jumper onto the bed as Nora laced the corset over her petticoat.

"Oh!" Lila gasped as Nora tugged on the ties.

"Sorry, miss," Nora apologized. "The corset will suck you in at the waist. Takes a good yank or two to get some definition."

"Boys seem to love Maggie," Lila observed. "I'm as thin as a reed, while Maggie has the most ladylike figure."

"You have your own appeal, even though it's different from hers."

Nora's words made Lila smile and she went to the mirror to admire her newly corseted figure. She looked so much older in the corset. It was high time that her mother realized she wasn't a child anymore and let her dress her age. "Could you help me put my hair up, Nora?"

"Your hair up?" Nora gasped. "What will your mother say?"

"She's so involved with marrying Maggie off that she won't even notice," Lila cajoled. "Please, Nora!"

"Well, maybe we could give it a try," Nora relented, skeptically. "Let me go get a box of hairpins from Maggie's room."

As soon as Nora departed, Lila walked over to the window. She knew it wasn't right to snoop, but she couldn't help it. Maggie and Teddy were now seated on a bench and Teddy was reading to Maggie from a book. From the love-struck expression on Teddy's handsome face—and the utter boredom emanating from Maggie—Lila guessed it was a book of love poems. Maggie had always hated love poems.

Teddy's attention was wasted on Maggie! Didn't she care a thing for his feelings? He was so wonderful— fun-loving

Abby Grahame

and clever. When they'd been out riding the other day, he'd gone off the trail only to reemerge further up, jumping out ahead of them on the path, grinning at their surprise. And the other night at dinner, when he'd told of the time while camping in South Africa that he'd been spooked by a herd of zebras, thinking they were ghosts in the night, he told it in such a hilarious way that she thought she'd die from laughing. If he ever paid even an iota of attention to Lila, even noticed she was there at all, Lila knew she would rain affection and tenderness on him that would make him fall forever in love with her.

As Lila watched, Maggie yawned. Had Teddy seen it? He had! Lila could tell from his crushed expression. That Maggie was plain mean. Lila had once looked up to her. Now she realized Maggie cared nothing for other people, only for her own amusement.

Most certainly mean-spiritedness accounted for Lila being left out of the trip to the Continent. Lila was certain her mother would have agreed to bring her along, but whenever Lila tried to bring it up Maggie voiced all sorts of objections. Lila got seasick. Lila was too young to attend the fancy balls. Lila would miss her school lessons. And all said as if Maggie was doing Lila a favor by forcing her to stay home! Was she really so dull that Maggie—who was only two years older—suddenly couldn't stand the idea of spending time with her?

"I've got the hairpins," Nora announced returning. "Now, how would you like it? Shall I roll it all toward the center like I do for your mother?".

"No! No! Too old-fashioned," Lila objected. "Can you do it in a knot on top with some wispy tendrils hanging loose?"

"It's a bit daring," Nora considered uncertainly.

"Oh, please." Lila crossed to Nora and sat on the cushioned stool by the mirror. "Mother and Father can't keep me looking like a child forever."

"All right," Nora agreed as she plucked up a hairbrush from the dresser and started brushing out Lila's hair. "But for the favor you have to tell me something. Is there a reason for this sudden interest in looking more ladylike?"

A burning sensation rose in Lila's cheeks and quick check of the mirror confirmed that she was blushing.

"If I tell you, promise not to laugh," Lila said.

"Promise," Nora declared.

Lila hesitated, then admitted in a rush, "Maggie doesn't care a thing for Teddy Fitzhugh and he's bound to tire of the way she treats him. Maybe, though, if I could manage to get his attention, he might fancy me, instead."

"Humph," Nora grunted.

"You promised not to laugh!" Lila exploded, mortified by Nora's reaction.

"Humph is not laughter," Nora insisted, still brushing. "I'm thinking is all."

"Thinking what?" Lila demanded with a petulant frown playing on her bow-shaped lips.

"Well, here's the thing. The other day I was coming upstairs when I heard Teddy standing in the upstairs hallway telling your sister that if she would agree to become engaged to him—"

"Engaged!" Lila cried. "Already? Why, that's outrageous! Why hasn't anyone told me about this?"

"Don't panic. She didn't agree. It seemed so hasty on his part. Maggie told him it was too soon and she would have to see how their feelings for each other developed. He didn't like it but he agreed."

"Why didn't she just tell him no? Anyone can see that

she has no feelings for him whatsoever. Oh, she's horrid!"

Nora twirled Lila's hair into a knot at the top of her head and starting pinning it into place. "She may have her reasons," Nora allowed.

Lila was so irritated she could barely sit still. "What reason could she possibly have?"

"That Teddy Fitzhugh is a sly one. He reminded her that he was about to come into a fantastic inheritance. More money, he says, than even the Duke of Cotswall. He points out that Wentworth Hall is in need of some serious repairs and says that if he and Maggie were betrothed he would feel it was his duty and obligation to preserve her ancestral home."

"See, that's how he is," Lila said, "sweet and willing to help."

"Sounds more like a bribe to me," Nora pointed out candidly.

Lila considered Nora's words. She just couldn't see Teddy that way. Teddy's offer wasn't a bribe but rather an inducement to love just as a man might bring flowers to the woman he was pursuing. "I think it's a lovely offer," Lila maintained. "Romantic, even. It's wrong for Maggie to mislead Teddy just so he can pay for repairs on the estate."

"He's already offered to pay to renovate the front entrance once the inheritance comes through. At first your father wouldn't hear of it but Teddy said it was the least he could do to repay your family's kindness to his sister and himself."

"She has no kindness or sense of decency," she said dismally.

"Oh, don't be so hard on your sister," Nora said. "She's doing what's best for the family."

"Maggie is only playing with Teddy because it strokes her vanity," Lila insisted.

"Aw, don't be bitter against your own sister," Nora counseled. With delicate finger work she coaxed small frills of hair out from Lila's hairline. "There. What do you think?" she asked.

Lila gazed at her new hairdo. It made her look grown-up, which was precisely what she'd wanted. Lila decided that her new hairstyle looked pretty and made her feel the same way. This was just the way to get Teddy to notice her.

"It's nearly dinnertime. You'd best get dressed," Nora said.

Lila glanced at the sailor jumper she'd tossed on the bed. "I can't put that jumper back on. It would look all wrong with the corset and new hair. Isn't there anything else I can wear, something more stylish?"

Arms folded thoughtfully, Nora considered Lila's request.

"There are two dresses that were ordered for Maggie before she went on her trip last year. She left before they were ready and she's never worn either of them. She says they're too prim for her taste, but I think they're beautiful frocks," Nora told Lila.

"Let me try them, please," Lila pleaded excitedly.

"I'll be right back," Nora said, heading for the door. "Wait here."

Lila turned in front of the mirror. The corset made her appeared more curvy than pudgy and Lila liked the way she looked in it despite its discomfort. It would be a small price to pay if her newly defined figure caught Teddy's attention.

"Look at you, all grown-up!" a female voice sounded.

Lila was mortified. Nora had forgotten to shut the door on her way out.

Crossing her arms modestly over her bare collarbone, Lila whirled around, startled to see Jessica Fitzhugh standing in the doorway grinning at her. In the girl's hand was the small red notebook she always seemed to be scribbling in. Lila had a diary too, but she didn't write in it in public. Seemed to defeat the purpose.

Jessica didn't wait to be invited but strolled in and sat on the edge of Lila's bed, depositing her notebook at her side. "Oh, don't be embarrassed," she chided. "You look smashing. It's about time, too. You couldn't go about in those little girl jumpers forever."

Although Lila could feel her cheeks burning, Jessica's words pleased her. "Do you think so? Really?"

"Positively," Jessica confirmed.

In the month that the Fitzhughs had been at Wentworth Hall, this was the first time Jessica had sat down to talk to her. Lila studied her there on the bed. Her auburn hair was piled high on her head and she wore a fashionable black tea-length skirt beneath a white blouse with balloon sleeves and a bow at the neck.

"With your hair up, you're every bit as pretty as your sister," Jessica went on.

"No one is as glamorous as Maggie," Lila protested glumly.

"My brother, Teddy, certainly thinks so," Jessica agreed with a sigh. "He's utterly abandoned me for her."

After her last disastrous conversation with Jessica, Lila had come to the conclusion that Jessica was just snooty and looked down on the Darlingtons since she and her brother were about to come into so much greater wealth. Now it struck Lila that maybe she had been right all along, that the girl was shy underneath her seeming brashness. People often mistook Lila's own shyness for snobbery. And perhaps she wasn't friendly because she'd always had her outgoing brother to lead the way. But now she was on her own.

"I know how you feel," Lila sympathized. "Ever since Maggie returned from her year abroad she's completely wrapped up in herself. It's as though she thinks she's grown and I'm only an insignificant child."

"Well, you don't look like a child right now," Jessica said.

"Here are the dresses I told you about," Nora said, entering the room with two dresses, one gray, the other a navy blue. "Try these." Nora stopped short when she noticed Jessica sitting there. "Hello, Miss Jessica."

Jessica stood up from the bed and approached Nora. "Let me see those dresses, Nora," she said, taking them from Nora and spreading them on the bed. "Dreadful," she pronounced.

"That's what Miss Maggie says, but I thought they were rather fetching," Nora disagreed.

"They were fetching two years ago," Jessica insisted. "Look at the length of them. They're to the floor! Everything is well above the ankle this year."

Jessica snapped up her red notebook with one hand and grabbed Lila by the wrist with the other. "Come to my room. I have some dresses I can lend you. We're about the same size."

Lila pulled back. "I can't go into the hallway. I'm not dressed."

Jessica yanked the pink satin cover from the bed and wrapped it around Lila's shoulders. "There! Good enough."

Lila felt wild and rebellious as she trailed Jessica down the hall in her bare feet covered only in the blanket. Once in the room, Jessica tossed her notebook down on her bed and flung open the door to her wardrobe. Extracting a silk dress of deep cobalt blue with a dropped waist and ruffled bottom, she held it up to Lila. "This would be divine on you and you wouldn't even need a corset."

Lila held the corset protectively. "No, I want the corset." She looked at herself in the mirror, dazzled at the prospect of wearing the gorgeous, stylish dress.

"Try it on," Jessica urged her.

When Lila had slipped the dress over her head, she spun in front of Jessica's gilded mirror, feeling unbelievably glamorous.

"You could wear it to dinner tonight," Jessica suggested.

"I could never," Lila protested, suddenly worried. "What if I got a food stain on it?"

Jessica laughed. "I've dropped food on it plenty of times. That's what servants are for."

"I suppose," Lila said, beaming at Jessica. It occurred to her that the two of them had a lot in common. They weren't far apart in age and they had both been recently abandoned by their closest sibling. Jessica could be a lot of fun. "I think we could become good friends, Jessica," Lila took the bold step of saying.

The expression of withdrawal in Jessica's eyes instantly made Lila wish she hadn't spoken. What had gone wrong?

"Yes, I hope we will be," Jessica agreed without an ounce of sincerity.

Why was she suddenly so against the idea of their friendship when she had been exuding camaraderie only moments ago? Was the term "friends" too much of a commitment? Had it reminded Jessica that she'd dropped her guard?

Lila glanced at the red notebook flung on the bed and, for a moment, thought she'd ask Jessica what she was always writing in it, but quickly reconsidered. It was probably too personal. Lila certainly wouldn't want anyone reading her diary.

"If you'll excuse me now, I need to go back to my journal writing," Jessica said with the faintest cold breeze in her voice.

Lila caught herself up, trying to return Jessica's sudden reserve with a distance of her own. She did not want to appear overeager. Still, maybe Jessica was simply fatigued and it was nothing personal.

"You write in your journal a good deal," Lila observed as she headed for the door.

"Hmm, I do," Jessica said, picking up the notebook.

"Yes, well . . . thanks for the loan of the dress. I'll have it washed, pressed, and back to you in no time."

"Keep it," Jessica said. "I'm done with it."

"I couldn't. I'll have it back to you," Lila insisted. At the door, she flashed a smile. A friendship with Jessica would be nice and it was too soon to give up on it altogether. "Enjoy your journal writing."

"Thank you," Jessica said politely. "I do find solace in my notebook."

"What a comfort it must be to you," Lila said.

Perhaps someday soon, when they knew each other better, Jessica would share its contents with her.

Chapter Eight

THAT EVENING NORA LAY ON HER NARROW bed in the servants' quarters, dressed in her maid's outfit, rubbing her bare feet. Was it possible that, at seventeen, her feet continued to grow? It certainly seemed that her shoes were pinching lately. Maybe they were simply swollen from being on them all day.

Helen came down the hall dressed in her plain white cotton nightgown, her orangey hair in a single braid down her back. She stopped by Nora's door, hovering outside. "Feet hurt?" she inquired.

"They're all swelled up," Nora reported, lifting them to show Helen.

Helen held her hands up, spreading her fingers. "With

me it's my hands. Having them in water so much of the day makes my cuticles crack. Hurts like crazy."

"My feet have only just started giving me trouble this month, since I have to tend to Jessica Fitzhugh in addition to my regular duties."

Helen leaned against the doorjamb casually. "Why don't they get her a maid of her own?"

"In this place? Cheapskate manor?" Nora asked with a laugh. "There's no money for that."

"Do you honestly believe there's no money, or is Lord Darlington just the tightest man who ever lived?"

Nora considered the question and decided that the money really wasn't there. The once brilliant colors of the Moorish style ballroom were faded and chipped. The leather couch in the upstairs smoking room had sustained a tear that was getting bigger by the day, yet the couch remained. Fixtures were broken, in places ceilings were coming down, tiles were chipped: The list went on and on. Surely those things would have been repaired if the Darlingtons had the money to do so. "They don't have it," Nora told Helen. "Just look around."

"Then why don't they move to a smaller place?" Helen questioned.

"Wentworth Hall has been in the Darlington family since the seventeen hundreds. They would never give it," Nora explained. "They're not like me and you, Helen. They're rich and they've always been rich. They can't stop being rich just because the money has run out."

"I don't understand," Helen admitted. "How can they be rich if they have no money?"

"It's breeding, Helen. Rich people have been marrying other rich people for so many generations that by now it's in their blood. They wouldn't know how to stop being rich."

Helen shook her head wearily. "I wish I knew how to stop being poor," she said. "It's never going to happen if I keep working here. A person can never get ahead when she earns only her room and board, medical expenses, and such a small amount of pay it's all gone by the middle of the week."

"I know," Nora commiserated. "By the time you post a letter and buy yourself a cup of tea, it's gone."

Helen yawned broadly as she stretched. "Well, better turn in. Another thrilling day of laundry awaits me in the morning."

"Sleep tight," Nora called after Helen as she disappeared down the hall.

A pang of hunger hit Nora, and the mention of tea made Nora crave a cup. The idea of getting back into her boots was unappealing, so she put on her woolen slippers and made her way down the servant's staircase to the kitchen.

The gas lamp glowed softly, and in its light Nora saw Michael hunched over a cup at the table. "Can't sleep?" she inquired, coming into the room and turning up the light.

"Naw. Can't," he admitted. "You?"

"I'm so tired I could sleep where I'm standing. Just a little hungry is all," Nora said as she lit a match to the stove burner. "Do you think we'll ever get electric lights in this place? Most neighboring estates have been wired for it."

"Being in this place is more and more like living back in the Dark Ages," Michael remarked gloomily.

"I agree with you there," Nora said, taking a cup down from the cupboard. "I'd hate to move on, though. It's like home. If anyone knows about that, it would be you. Remember when we used to play out in the back with

Wesley, Maggie, and Lila? We were all friends then and it didn't make a difference who was a servant and who wasn't."

"That was a long time ago," Michael said.

"Not so long. It's not like we're ancient now," Nora pointed out.

"Well, it seems long ago," Michael insisted. "And even then we'd have to sneak about. Lord and Lady Darlington would have sent us packing if they knew we'd been out playing with their children."

The teakettle whistled and Nora turned off the flame. "What's keeping you awake, Michael?" She sat down beside him with her tea.

"I'm worrying about having a job," Michael told her. "The family barely goes riding anymore and they don't need a whole stable. I'm only nineteen years old and already I'm a dying breed."

Nora patted his arm. "It can't be as bad as all that."

"It is!" Michael insisted. "Horses are expensive to take care of and they would bring a lot of money if they were sold."

"Hmm," Nora replied. Michael was feeling so gloomy

that she didn't think that this was the right time to tell him about the letter she'd picked up from Lady Darlington's desk the other day. It was from the Darlingtons' eldest son, twenty-year-old Wesley, who had gone off to school at Oxford. He was returning home from America, where he'd been since the end of the school year, and bringing along his American friend before going back to university. Upon his return for the remainder of the summer, one thing he hoped to accomplish, according to his letter, was to enlist Lady Darlington's help in persuading Lord Darlington to take certain measures to make Wentworth Hall profitable once more, inspired by what he saw while he was in America. One of his ideas was to sell off pieces of the estate. The letter hadn't explicitly mentioned the stable, but it stood to reason the horses and the groom were on the chopping block.

"What does *hmm* mean?" Michael asked.

"Nothing. I'm just listening to you is all. They'd never let you go, Michael. You've been here your entire life, and your father and grandfather before you. They would find a place for you."

"It might be for the good," Michael said. "If I get free

Ally Grahame

of this place, maybe I could make my way in the world, make something of myself instead of always being a servant. I couldn't leave my father behind, though."

"What would you do?" Nora asked.

"I don't know. That's the thing. Maybe I could go down to the racetrack and become a trainer. One thing I know is horses."

"That you do," Nora agreed. "Nobody better with a horse. But isn't the racetrack a bit . . . disreputable?"

"Why should I care about that?" Michael challenged. "It's not like I have some big reputation to protect. If I could earn some real money, nobody would care how I got it."

"By 'nobody' do you mean Maggie?" Nora probed.

"No, I don't," Michael said. "I've barely spoken to Maggie since she's been back and that's nearly two months now. She's forgotten me and I've left her behind as well."

Nora sighed, not believing a word of it. Maggie might have moved on from Michael, but he was as stuck on her as ever. Any fool could see that.

"I know what you mean about not being a servant forever," Nora said, intentionally changing the subject. "I plan to put money aside until I have enough to open a little tea shop of my own."

"That sounds nice, Nora, but how can you put anything aside with the pittance they pay you here? We're little more than serfs living on the estate like in the feudal times."

Smiling confidently, Nora tapped her forehead. "I have a plan and I've already begun. I've been taking on extra sewing jobs."

"From who?" Michael asked.

"People in town," Nora explained. "I've put up little signs in town and the jobs have already begun coming in. I pick them up and drop them off on my half-day off."

"So you never have a moment when you're not working," Michael observed.

"I don't mind. It's going to bring me a better future. I don't want to be sitting in this kitchen like Rose or Mrs. Howard when I'm their age."

"Like my dad, working here in the garden all these years," Michael agreed. "He'd never leave Wentworth Hall, and he's getting on in years. I don't know how he'd feel if I left the place. It's part of what keeps me here."

"Oh!" Therese startled at the sight of Michael and

Abby Grahame

Nora as she entered the room. "I didn't expect anyone to be awake so late," she said. She was wrapped in a floral robe with pleated lace at the sleeves and delicate blue satin slippers. Her abundant blond curls were loosely tied in a ribbon. "I will go," she added, backing up.

"No, no," Michael said. "Come join the ranks of the sleepless and bothered."

"Pull up a chair," Nora seconded the invitation. Nora didn't yet trust Therese but maybe she wouldn't feel that way if she got to know her better. "So what's keeping you up this night?" she inquired.

Therese sighed deeply. "They want me to start teaching the girls French in addition to my nanny duties," she revealed. "I know how to speak French, of course, but I'm not sure I can teach someone else to speak the language. I was hired to take care of the baby, not to be a teacher. What if I fail? I will have to return to Paris."

Something about Therese's response didn't ring true to Nora. Therese was clearly bothered by something. But what? "Why did you want to leave France?" Nora asked, hoping she would learn some scandalous secret. Was there a ruined love affair? A crime?

"My mother," Therese replied. "She died last year and Paris holds too many memories of her. Everything reminded me of our happy times together. I thought time would ease those memories. But I needed distance, too. And then I got the offer from Lady Darlington and it seemed perfect."

Nora probed further. "What about your father? Where is he?"

"I never knew my father," Therese revealed. "As I've mentioned, my mother worked at Lord Darlington's sister's estate. She never revealed to anyone who my father was. She just felt lucky that Lady Daphne let her keep her job despite her condition."

"What a scandal!" Nora said, pleased to have unearthed a juicy detail. "Was everyone shocked?"

"The French are not as easily shocked as the English," Therese commented. "And Lady Daphne was always kind to her. And to me. When Lady Darlington arrived from Nice with James, Lady Daphne acted as my reference."

Nora patted Therese's hand. "So, you're a penniless orphan like me, poor thing."

"Yes, but I hope to make money working here," Therese said.

"Ha!" Nora barked with laughter. "Good luck."

"You're not earning very much, are you?" Michael asked.

"I have no expenses," Therese said with a shrug. "Still, Wentworth Hall is not what I expected. I thought I would start a new life here . . . but I do not see any way for it to begin."

"We know how you feel," Michael commiserated.

Therese yawned, covering her mouth. "I should check on James," she decided. "He wakes in the night and her ladyship does not hear him. She is a sound sleeper."

Getting up, Therese bid them good night and departed.

"Nice girl," Michael remarked after Therese was gone.

"Hmm," Nora responded.

"What? Don't you think so?"

"Do you believe that story about Paris having too many memories of her mother?"

"Why shouldn't I?" Michael asked.

Nora gave him a look, getting up to bring her teacup to the sink. "If she has such happy memories of her mother, why wouldn't she want to be near them? Has she no friends or family in Paris that she'd want to stay close to?"

Michael laughed out loud. "Your mind certainly runs overtime, Nora. Forget your tea shop, you should set up as a private detective."

"Not a bad idea, Michael. Maybe you and I could be partners."

Michael stretched and pushed his chair back. "Not a chance, Nora. The less I know about people and their dirty little secrets, the happier I am."

"You're wrong there," Nora disagreed, returning her washed cup to the cupboard. "Knowledge is power."

Nora said good night to Michael and headed back up the servants' staircase. The tea and conversation had made her feel more alert instead of ready to sleep. She decided to work on some sewing but, arriving in her room, she realized she'd left her mending basket in one of the second-floor guest rooms. No one ever used this one—due to excessive water stains on the ceiling plaster, which made the room an excellent place to escape to when things were quiet.

Heading for the room, Nora was struck by how immense and quiet the estate seemed at night. Moonlight beamed through the high arched and mullioned windows, lighting her way down the high-ceilinged corridors with their gleaming marble floors and bouncing its white glow off gilded mirrors and heavy crystal chandeliers. How grand this place must have been in its heyday! It was majestic with a decaying, kind of antique charm.

It was more like a palace than a home. As much as Nora dreamed of leaving the service, there were other moments when she was glad for the warmth and coziness of the downstairs kitchen and the low-ceilinged servants' quarters. To inhabit Wentworth Hall was like living in a vast impersonal museum, full of artifacts but lacking any sense of hominess.

As Nora neared the guest room door, she was shocked to see that light was emanating from the space at the bottom of another guest room door. At this hour? Who could be in there?

Approaching noiselessly and with caution, Nora crept to the door and listened. She recognized the voices immediately: Maggie and Teddy Fitzhugh were engaged in an impassioned argument.

"If that's how you feel, why then did you agree to meet me for a tryst in the middle of the night?" Teddy asked in a voice bristling with anger and wounded pride.

"I've told you!" Maggie cried, exasperated. Nora could picture the girl throwing her arms wide. "I thought I could force myself to have feelings for you. I've tried! But I simply can't feel what I don't feel."

"And can you force yourself to entertain feelings with a doddering duke more than twice your age?" Teddy came back at her angrily.

Maggie was silent, then said softly, "I don't know."

"I have as much money, probably more, than he has. And I'm a great deal younger. How can you compare the two of us? There's not even a contest."

"This is not a competition! I don't want him, either. I don't even know him and he doesn't know me. It's absurd. Father is only entertaining the idea because he wants to make an advantageous connection with a wealthy man. He's using me as a pawn and I don't want that. It's why I tried to love you, Teddy. I wish I could love you. For a while I thought I could."

"You are a liar!" Teddy accused her. "You've been stringing me along for over a month now and you never returned my love."

"I wasn't toying with you. Honestly. I was trying my best to learn to love you," Maggie explained.

"Because you saw it would be advantageous to love me?"

"Yes! It would suit everyone if I could return your affection—but I don't. I have to be honest with myself and with you. I simply do not love you. It's out of my control."

"And am I so impossible to love?"

Nora cringed at the hurt in his voice. At the moment he was not the pompous peacock she'd become used to seeing strutting around the estate with an air of condescension. He was a lovesick pup who was having his dreams dashed.

"Someone will find you easy to love," Maggie said, her voice growing kinder. "It's just not me."

"I wish you had told me all this a month ago before I made a fool of myself over you. My sister was right about you," Teddy snarled, enraged.

"Jessica? What did she have to do with all this?"

"She cautioned me against you—not that I would listen. She even tried to parade your slip of a sister before me to distract my affections. To prove it was not love that I felt, but blind infatuation. But I was too besotted to see what everyone else must have known all along."

"I'm sorry, Teddy," Maggie said, her voice cracking.

"Not as sorry as I am," Teddy snapped back.

Nora jumped, flattening against the wall, as the door banged open and Teddy blew out of the smoking room, storming down the hall. Nora sank back into the shadows along the wall. "Nor as sorry as you will be, Maggie Darlington," she heard him mutter.

Peering into the crack of the open door, Nora saw Maggie sink into the ripped leather couch, weeping.

Nora decided to let Maggie have her moment of grief in private. When she was sure that Teddy was gone, she scampered back down the dark, moonlit hall to her room.

Abby Grahame

MAGGIE STOOD ON THE MEZZANINE FLOOR, observing the stately dancers moving on the gleaming marble floor of the Duke of Cotswall's ballroom below. A quadrille was really such an old-fashioned, formal type of dance. It had its own beauty, she supposed, but it wasn't for her.

The women all wore the same off-the-shoulder kind of gown, nipped tightly at the waist with a wide flowing skirt below. Lady Darlington had insisted that Maggie take off the kimono-style dress with the flowing overdress and matching headpiece that she'd planned to wear. Now she tugged on the loathed taffeta corset she wore beneath her plum-colored, crepe de chine gown. It was cutting under her breasts and squeezing her rib cage.

The men were dressed in black tails and trousers. With erect posture they stepped back and forth, promenading with their lady partners: hands held high, chins tipped up, smiles frozen in place.

Quaint and pleasant as the dancers were, Maggie's eyes were not on them. Instead they were fixed on Teddy Fitzhugh, who had glued himself to her father's side this evening. More worrisome than that was the expression on Teddy's face whenever he laid eyes on her. At those times his expression glowed with triumphant mockery, his mouth twisting into a tight smile. Maggie didn't like it. Some treachery was being enacted; if only she could figure out what he was up to.

Not that Teddy didn't have a right to be upset with her. She hadn't meant to lead him on the way she had. She had tried with her whole heart to love him. She just couldn't do it. Even when she was trying to do right, it ended up so wrong.

She took another step back from the banister. For the moment, she seemed to be eluding her father's gaze up here on the mezzanine tucked behind a mosaic-covered pillar. Maggie ducked back even farther as the Duke of

Cotswall joined Teddy and Lord Darlington. The sight of their wealthy next-door neighbor with his protruding ears, rotund belly, and double chins sent a chill through her. Was her father insane?! Did he really expect her to consider marrying this toad of a man?

In a heart-stopping gesture, Teddy pointed up to the mezzanine, pointing out Maggie's whereabouts to the duke and Lord Darlington. Had he realized she was there all along? Pivoting swiftly, Maggie attempted to look as though she was gazing in another direction and completely unaware of their attention.

Maggie turned and hurried away in search of a new hiding spot. Spying a side door down a short flight of stairs, she headed for it and found herself suddenly sprung free into the sultry summer night. What a relief!

"Have you made a clean escape?"

Maggie's head swung toward the familiar voice. "Michael!" she gasped before she could stop herself. In his groom's uniform with its short military-style jacket and form-fitting pants over tall, well-polished boots, he was, by far, the most dashingly handsome man at Cotswall Manor that night.

"You're looking very beautiful tonight," Michael remarked, almost begrudgingly. With similar hesitation, he began walking toward her. The overhead outside gas lanterns shimmered on his dark hair and she felt again that familiar pang of longing he had elicited within her. When had their childhood camaraderie transformed into this other feeling? The truth was, she could no longer recall a time she hadn't loved him. And why couldn't she make this wanting stop, no matter how much she tried? Despite all that had happened . . . ?

"It was a bore in there," Maggie attempted to explain as he joined her.

"Then stay here with me."

His green eyes fixed on her in a way that made her move toward him in an involuntary sway. When he was near, she felt like a plant inclining toward the sun. But those green eyes also served as a reminder . . . she had to stay strong. It was the only right thing to do now.

"Maggie, listen," Michael spoke in a firm, gentle voice. "The other day didn't go very well between us but I only want to understand why—"

"There you are!" Teddy called, coming through the

Abby Graheme

side door. "I thought I saw you leave through here."

The duke and her father followed as Teddy came to her side. With a darting glance, she watched Michael walk off, disappearing into the darkness. As the two men drew close, she forced a smile to her lips.

"Teddy!" she cooed as though he were a welcome sight. "You've found me. I came out here for some air and to admire the lovely gardens."

"Not as lovely as you, yourself," Teddy said smoothly.

Oh, how she loathed him at this moment, so smug and pleased that he had her trapped. She'd been right not to take his claims of love seriously. How could he have really loved her so recently and resort to this now?

The heavyset duke's small, dark, bright eyes bore into her. Bowing at the waist, the duke reached for her hand. Willing herself not to flinch, Maggie extended her hand to be kissed. Although she knew the duke to be an avid hunter, his hands were disconcertingly soft, almost feminine, a thing Maggie found repugnant in a man. His kiss left a wet mark on her hand, which she forced herself not to wipe away as she withdrew it. "Are you enjoying the quadrille, Duke?" she asked politely.

"Please, call me Edmund," the duke replied. "And yes, I am enjoying myself immensely. I thank you for the invitation, for Mr. Fitzhugh here has informed me that it was you who extended it."

How she wanted to strangle Teddy!

"We are neighbors, after all," Maggie said, trying to mitigate the situation by making it known that neighborly obligation was what had motivated her, and nothing more scintillating.

"We have not seen nearly enough of each other," Edmund Marlborough replied in a tone that Maggie found oily and unctuous.

"We certainly will be seeing much more of you, Edmund," Lord Darlington said with warmth.

"Would you and your family accept my invitation to lunch tomorrow?" Edmund asked Lord Darlington.

"We would be delighted," Lord Darlington replied.

This was getting out of hand. The intent way the duke was gazing at her was making her flesh crawl. Maybe she shouldn't have been so quick to rebuff Teddy. At the very least he was her age and handsome. "Lunch tomorrow might not be good for me," Maggie said. "Teddy and I always take our stroll at that time, don't we, Teddy?" This was almost true. They used to take a lunchtime stroll but since their blowup three nights earlier they had not. If the duke thought she was involved with a man more her age, he might back off.

"I won't be able to stroll with you anymore," Teddy put in quickly.

"Really? Has there been a change in our plans?" she bluffed. She hadn't expected him to turn on her so completely. Not to the point of out and out rudeness.

"No, I won't be strolling with you anymore ever, I'm afraid," Teddy continued. "The business of my upcoming inheritance will require my full attention from now on." With a sharp bow Teddy bade the men good-bye and walked off.

Lord Darlington looked perplexed. "Poor boy must be feeling the pressure of having to run his late father's empire. He is not normally so brusque."

"Young men are so fickle in their . . . pursuits," Edmund remarked evenly.

"Yes" was all Maggie could think of to say. She shifted uncomfortably from one foot to the other, unable to think of a new plan, especially with the duke and her father right there staring so expectantly at her.

Edmund offered her his bent elbow. "I heard you have recently been abroad," he began. "Tell me your impressions of Paris. It's been several years since I have been there."

He smelled of the heavy pomade he'd used to slick his thinning hair over the bald top of his head. "Did you attend the Opera House?" he asked.

"No, I never got there," Maggie replied.

"I adore opera," the duke said as he strolled with her and Lord Darlington.

"The theater must be grand, I suppose," Maggie answered. "I've never quite understood opera."

"You must try it!" the duke said to her. "The opera is thrilling." He went on at great length as they descended the stairs, telling her of last season's operas and their various plots. Maggie felt as though she was attending a classical music appreciation class.

The duke steered them back toward the side door from which she'd exited, and guided her down onto an ornate outside bench of wrought iron. "We can enjoy the lovely evening here together if you like."

Abby Grahame

Trapped! There was not a chance of escaping from him now. How pleased Teddy must be! At least her father was still with them. Her mother would have abandoned her with this catch long ago!

"You two chat and get to know each other better," Lord Darlington cut in. "I need to check something with Lady Darlington."

Drat!

Maggie had no choice but to sit and listen to Edmund continue on regarding his early days as a young opera fan. Her nostrils flared as she suppressed waves of yawning.

A servant burst from the side door, a look of alarm on his face. "Sir," he addressed Edmund urgently. "Your horse is galloping loose on the grounds. Somehow he jumped the paddock fence where he was being cooled!"

Edmund leaped up, seeming to forget Maggie entirely, and rushed back inside behind his servant.

Maggie stood, straining to see out onto the grounds beyond the circle of lights cast by the estate's lanterns. She discerned large forms moving in the darkness and detected the pounding of hoofbeats off in the distance.

"Michael," she whispered to herself. Thrilled by the

idea, she realized only Michael could have—would have—done such a thing. He'd done it to free her from Teddy and from Edmund. Michael—her hero even when she didn't deserve one.

Lila gathered the rose-colored silk of her gown. Her dress was not the gorgeous off-the-shoulder affairs the grown women wore—her mother had forbidden that—but a dress she was happy with nonetheless, with a shawl neckline. She was pleasantly amazed at how unopposed her parents had been to her more mature makeover. Perhaps they simply accepted it was the right time, though a darker part of Lila suspected that they were just too distracted with their own lives—her mother with James and marrying off Maggie, and her father with Wentworth Hall—to take much notice.

The quadrille had become quite dull since a large population of the male guests had run off to help the Duke of Cotswall retrieve his carriage horse that was now galloping free across his fields. How happy and eager the men had been to shed their formal coats and go out to help recapture the escaped horse. What a stroke of luck for Maggie! Evil as Maggie had been since her return, even Lila pitied her sister having to duck the attentions of a man nearly as old as their own father.

Lila had noticed that Jessica had disappeared from the ball and now headed for the outside garden. It was pretty clear that Teddy's affections for Maggie had been rebuffed. The two of them hadn't even spoken for the last three days and Teddy was in a foul mood, all scowls and growls. Hopefully that would pass in time. Finally this was Lila's chance to make him forget about her haughty sister. If only she could catch his attention. Perhaps Jessica could help her with that.

When Lila was near Jessica's room, she saw that the door was open and the girl had seated herself on a bench facing the Duke's famed beautiful rose bushes. The fashionable deep red gown she'd worn during her brief appearance at the quadrille seemingly matched the budding blooms. Her auburn hair was bound up in an elaborate twist of braids and curls. Lila thought she looked gorgeous.

Since their friendly conversation of the week before, the one that had suddenly turned sour at the end, Jessica seemed to be avoiding her. Lila was mystified by what had happened. It seemed to coincide with Teddy losing interest in Maggie. So many secrets inside Wentworth Hall, and as usual, Lila was in the dark about all of them.

With a light step toward her, Lila coughed to get her attention.

Startled, Jessica twisted toward Lila and pouted at the sight of her. "Oh, hello, Lila. Bored of the ball?"

Lila presumed to settle lightly at the end of the bench. "The men have run off to catch a runaway horse," Lila reported.

Jessica shut the red notebook she'd been writing in, slipping it into her purse, and straightened. "You people can't even throw an intriguing ball, can you?" she complained. "The men in this neighborhood would rather catch a horse than flirt with the pretty girls. What a pack of rubes."

Stung, Lila scowled at her. "'You people'? I suppose the gentry are so much more fascinating in South Africa," she snapped.

"No, not in Johannesburg, though we have our share of darlings. The place where they're really suave is London," Jessica declared.

At the mention of London, Lila decided to bite back

the instinct to match Jessica's peevish tone. "You've been to London?" she asked.

"During this past spring season: Father wanted Teddy and me to meet some of society's best, so he brought us over. He had his fatal heart attack at one of the season's fanciest balls given by one of the best families in London. That's how we happened to come to you. We wouldn't have come all the way here from South Africa. Our father's solicitor, who has our money held hostage right now, insisted that we come here until we turn eighteen. It's so dreadful."

"Is it really so awful?" Lila challenged, her temper rising. "Hasn't everyone been nice to you here?"

"It's not that," Jessica allowed. "It's simply so dull here."

Lila stood up, deeply annoyed. Jessica's implication was that Lila—the only one who had attempted to be friendly to Jessica—was too dreadfully dull for words. Lila felt foolish for ever believing Jessica could be a friend to her, or an ally in trying to win Teddy's affection. Would she think it was hilarious for poor hopelessly boring Lila to set her cap for the fascinating and incredibly wealthy Teddy Fitzhugh?

"Thank heavens I have this notebook to write in or I'd go mad," Jessica continued. "There's not even an interesting novel in the entire library. Believe me, I've searched."

She couldn't fault Jessica for that last statement. Lila had often thought the same thing herself. Lila wandered to the edge of the patio and looked out over the moonlit field. She strained to hear any sign of the runaway coach horse or the men. Lila was about to turn away when she spied movement in front of the stable.

Under the beam of the overhead stable lantern, Michael stood talking to Maggie, who looked like a figure out of a romantic painting. The skirt of her gown was caught up over one arm, and her soft blond hair was coming unfurled from its silver combs.

Lila leaned closer to the glass. What were they talking about? Was Maggie smiling? It was a smile Lila remembered from long ago but hadn't seen in over a year. Michael was leaning toward Maggie.

In the glow of the lanterns, Michael looked devastatingly handsome. In fact, Michael and Maggie made a gorgeous couple. It was a scandalous thought! Lila almost laughed out loud at the idea.

Abby Grahame

Regardless of what they were talking about, they seemed to be having much more fun than Lila was. Maybe they wouldn't mind her joining the conversation.

"Where are you going?" Jessica asked, looking up from the writing to which she'd returned.

As Lila dashed across the lawn, she looked over her shoulder at Jessica. "I think I will see what's happening with that horse," she said.

Chapter Ten

MICHAEL GAZED INTO MAGGIE'S BROWN eyes and every feeling he had been denying came rushing back. How he'd missed her!

"When I saw you needed some help, releasing the duke's horse was the only thing I could think of," Michael told her. "It was a bit drastic, but it worked."

"Absolutely! It worked like a charm. I can't thank you enough," she replied, laughter in those lively eyes. "Are you sure the horse won't come to harm?"

"Very certain," Michael assured her. "It will gallop across the fields, enjoy its bit of freedom, and then head back for its stall. It knows the way back. The men know it as well. They're making a big show of finding it but I think they're just enjoying a little freedom too."

This made Maggie laugh hard. The sound of it made Michael's heart leap. It had been so long.

"So everyone is in this plot together," she concluded. "It's just that no one will admit what's really going on."

"Something like that," Michael agreed, the smile fading from his lips. "It's somewhat like what's going on with you."

Maggie also became serious. "I don't know what you mean."

"Don't you?"

"No."

"I mean that you're angry with me and I don't know why."

Maggie turned her back on him. "I was, but it doesn't matter anymore."

"Because you've moved on?" Michael asked.

"You were right, Michael," Maggie told him. "I couldn't accept it at the time but I've grown up since then."

"Don't do this, Maggie," Michael urged. Maybe he was being rash, he knew. But the chances to be alone with her were so few and far between. He had to say his piece, especially now when she wasn't shutting him out. "That night before you left, I only said I didn't love you because I thought it was impossible between us. I didn't want to hurt you; I actually thought I was helping you by setting you free from a love that could never be. But since you've been gone I've realized it was pride and false nobility on my part. I've grown too. I know now that we belong together. Whatever it takes." Michael was surprised to find he meant it. He had fooled himself into believing he could go on without Maggie. Finally being able to talk to her—to tell her all the things he'd meant to the moment she got back, before the weeks she'd spent ignoring him for Teddy—unleashed his true feelings.

"I love you, Maggie Darlington," Michael continued. "I've probably loved you my whole life, before I even knew what it meant to be in love with someone. When we are together, I feel more myself than I have ever felt. I am not Michael the groom, or Michael the gardener's son, I'm just Michael. And you are not Lady Margaret. You are Maggie. The most beautiful, sweet girl in the world. The girl who can squeeze more happiness and life out of one day than most folks can in a lifetime. Come back to me, Maggie."

When Maggie turned back toward him, tears brimmed in her eyes. "Then you should have said all that at the time. Before I left for France. It's too late now, Michael."

"Listen to me. I have a plan. I'm going to go to the racetrack and find work as a horse trainer."

"When are you planning to do that?" Maggie asked, looking shocked.

"I'm not sure yet. When the time is right. Soon."

For a moment he thought Maggie seemed interested, but her face crumpled once more. "Don't speak any more, Michael. It's no use. Too much has happened!"

"What? What has happened?" Michael asked passionately. Maggie opened her mouth to speak and then seemed to think better of it "It's too late! It's too late!" she wailed, tears spilling over onto her cheeks.

"Tell me why!" Michael implored.

"It just is," Maggie insisted. "Things have changed! Changed forever!"

"But what has changed?" he begged to know.

"Life!" Maggie cried, throwing her arms wide.

Even in her pain and misery, this was the Maggie he knew, full of feeling, not the ice queen she was trying so desperately to be. He reached out and held her by the shoulders, wanting to pull her close as he had so many times before, to protect and love her.

Maggie gazed up at him, her tear-stained eyes filled with longing, but then she broke free, running off into the darkness outside their circle of lantern light, her gown rustling as she fled.

Michael took a step forward to go after her but decided against it. Silently he cursed himself for ever telling Maggie he didn't love her. What a fool he'd been! He had been so certain he was doing the right thing at the time.

How desperately he wished he could take it all back. He should have told her, instead, that he wouldn't be a horse groom all his life, that he would work hard and do whatever it took to advance his station in life. While he could never reproduce the grandeur of Wentworth Hall, he could promise her a decent life.

If only. If only.

Something moved off in the darkness and Michael turned sharply toward the sound.

Lila! How long had she been standing there?

"Lila!" he called, but she was gone.

* * *

Nora sat at the big round kitchen table, hemming a velvet ball gown, still in her maid's uniform. After all the excitement of preparing the girls for the quadrille she was wide-awake and couldn't sleep. The red fabric she was working with was luscious but difficult to get a needle through. The satin and crinoline hems underneath it would be easier.

Despite the challenges of the fabric, she was happy for the job. She'd charge for three hems separately. And all because the wearer of the gown insisted on wearing flat satin slippers so she wouldn't be taller than the young gentleman she'd set her sights on.

Nora was so pleased to think of the money her side jobs were bringing in. Eventually, she might have enough to leave service and work for herself! Maybe even before she was let go for lack of funds at Wentworth Hall. That destiny seemed to be encroaching at a rapid rate.

"Oh, you're up!" Therese entered the kitchen looking sleepy-eyed and wrapped in her robe, her blond hair braided down the back.

"Always up," Nora confirmed. "I'm not a big sleeper."

"Is that household mending?" Therese asked. "Do they

work you so hard that you must sew through the night?"

Nora smiled. "No, this is my escape plan. I'm saving extra money to buy my own tearoom someday. But you mustn't tell. It's against the rules and I could get sacked for doing it."

Therese put her finger to her lip. "Not a word," she assured Nora.

"Why are you up?" Nora inquired as she snapped a piece of thread with her teeth.

"Oh, the poor baby will not settle. It is his teeth, I am sure. I have come to get the frozen bread for James and a cup of warm milk for her ladyship who was awakened by the crying and can not fall back to sleep," Therese explained as she took the bread from the icebox.

"You bring the baby the soother," Nora said, laying aside her mending. "The poor tyke must be in agony. He shouldn't be made to wait. I'll bring her ladyship the milk."

"Thank you so much, Nora," Therese said, hurrying off with the frozen bread.

After heating the milk and pouring it into a silver teapot along with a white bone china cup and saucer, Nora arranged a teaspoon and a lace-trimmed white linen napkin on a silver tray and headed up to Lady Darlington's third-floor bedroom,

Abby Grahame

balancing it all on the tray. As she neared the bedroom door, she hesitated because she heard Lord Darlington speaking within, and his voice was decidedly agitated.

"What good is having a nanny if she can't keep the child quiet at night?" Lord Darlington complained. "I am exhausted after this evening's commotion and I do not need to be awakened by the wail of a peevish child."

"I'm so sorry, dear," Lady Darlington apologized sleepily. "Go back to bed. Therese is in with the baby now and I don't hear him anymore. You shan't be disturbed again, I hope."

"'I hope'?" Lord Darlington barked.

"Well, one can't be one hundred percent sure with a baby, can one?"

"How you ever got pregnant at your age, I can't imagine," Lord Darlington went on.

"Nor can I, but it happened just the same," Lady Darlington said blandly. "And he's a dear little fellow."

"I already have one son, I really didn't need another," Lord Darlington grumbled.

"Arthur!" Lady Darlington scolded, shocked at his coldness.

"I'm only saying what's true. Another baby is another mouth to feed and child to clothe, another boy who has to be educated. And a nanny to feed and clothe along with him."

"I don't understand your dislike of Therese," Lady Darlington replied. "You didn't seem to mind her at first. I can't help but feel she's done something to upset you."

"She can't keep the damn baby quiet for one!" Lord Darlington snapped.

Lady Darlington sighed. "It's late, we can talk about this another time."

"You have put me off before, Beatrice. I'd like you to let Therese go. Send her back to France."

Still listening at the door, Nora set down her tray so she could lean closer to hear better. "I don't understand why," Lady Darlington said, sounding aghast at the request. Nora felt the same. Why was Lord Darlington getting involved in an issue traditionally left to his wife?

"I would prefer an English nanny."

Nora twisted her mouth skeptically. She didn't believe him. The stiffness of his tone made her feel he was lying.

"You've said that before. But we've enlisted Therese to teach French to the girls," Lady Darlington reminded him.

"A useless language, if you ask me," Lord Darlington insisted.

"Knowledge of French is considered a sign of good breeding in a wife," Lady Darlington replied. "In fact, isn't Maggie's time spent abroad part of what sparked the duke's interest in her?"

"Interest means nothing without a proper offer for her hand. And regardless, I prefer an English nanny for my son. Do you want James sounding like an affected and foppish lad with a French accent?"

"He won't have a French accent, but he will be bilingual. Which is an asset in business endeavors, as you know."

"What, you expect a son of mine to engage in trading? He will have plenty of work on his hands helping his elder brother manage Wentworth Hall. And please don't change the subject. I said I want her gone and I will not be trifled with!" Lord Darlington exploded. With that he stormed from the room, not even noticing Nora, who was flattened against the wall. She seemed to be doing that a lot lately.

A sob caught in Lady Darlington's throat. Gathering up her tray, Nora rushed in.

Lady Darlington sat at her vanity in her lavender satin robe, her long salt-and-pepper hair loose to her shoulders, with her face buried in her hands. Her shoulders shook as she cried silent tears.

"I have your warm milk, your ladyship," Nora spoke tenderly. In spite of Lady Darlington's pretense and occasional haughtiness, Nora liked the woman and hated to see her so upset. "Have some. You'll feel better."

Lady Darlington looked up, surprised to see Nora. "Why are you up so late, Nora?" she asked, wiping away her tears.

"I couldn't sleep after the excitement of the ball," Nora told a half-truth.

"I see." Lady Darlington poured herself some milk, which Nora was relieved to see continued to steam slightly.

There was an awkward pause as Nora waited, hoping Lady Darlington would engage her in discussion regarding what had just passed with her husband. "Thank you, Nora, and good night" was all she said.

"Good night, your ladyship," Nora replied, dipping into a quick curtsy.

Nora burst from the room, dying to tell someone what

Abby Grahame

she had just heard. The only one possibly awake, though, was Therese. Should she tell Therese? Maybe it would blow over and she would be upsetting her needlessly. On the other hand, if she was about to get the sack, she should be warned.

When Nora entered the kitchen, Therese was there, sitting at the table, yawning but awake. Her half-closed eyes widened at the sight of Nora. "What happened?" she asked, seeing Nora's excited expression.

"Oh . . ." Nora hesitated, making up her mind what to do. "Lady Darlington was having a heated discussion with his lordship," she reported, gathering up the gown she'd been hemming.

"So he was up," Therese surmised. "That's when he must have dropped this." She took an opened envelope from the pocket of her robe and placed it on the table. It was addressed to Lord Arthur Darlington from his solicitor in London.

"What is it?" Nora asked. "You didn't read it, did you?"

A mischievous sparkle came into Therese's eyes. "Of course I did. Wouldn't you?"

Nora had to grin. "Naturally."

Therese took the paper from the envelope and handed it to Nora.

Nora scanned the letter and quickly gleaned the meaning of its contents. Lord Darlington had contacted his lawyer in London about selling off not only large tracts of land on his estate—including the stable and its horses—but also many of the family's most prized heirlooms.

After reading the letter, Nora looked at Therese with a stunned expression. "I had no idea things were this bad," she remarked honestly. "It's worse than I thought."

"Do you think our positions here are at risk?" Therese asked in a worried tone.

Nora nodded her head. There was no sense warning Therese about what she had just overheard. This was warning enough. And Therese might not be the only one who would soon be hunting for a position, it seemed. It was possible that before long the entire staff of Wentworth Hall might be seeking new employment.

Chapter Eleven

The Sussex Courier

THE FURTHER ADVENTURES OF . . .
THE WORTHLESS SAGA

Presenting part two of the popular
ongoing new series . . .
"Pack My Jewels. We're Moving to the Poorhouse."

It was quite the scene at our favorite broken-
down palace earlier this week.

"Sell! Sell! Sell!" cried Lord Worthless as he
stood in the immense front foyer of Faded
Glory Manor, his family's once grand estate.

"Everything must go!"

Moving men carried out furniture and racks of gowns, jewels, and fur coats, all to be sold at an auction in London. Lady Worthless hurried out with a wailing baby slung over her shoulder. Ignoring the baby's cries, she tugged at a fox stole at the top of a pile the mover is carrying out. "Not Foxie!" she cried. As she pulled, dust rises in the air. "He once belonged to Mumsie and her Mumsie before her. You simply can't take Foxie."

"Sorry, lady. His Nibs over there told us to take everything," the moving man said.

The baby crawled to the top of Lady Worthless's upswept hair and sat there crying. Lady Worthless bawled just as loudly over the loss of her beloved Foxie. The baby finally stopped crying and sucked his thumb. Lady Worthless followed suit.

A mover came out with one of the maids slung over his shoulder. She beat on his shoulders, bellowing. "You can't take me! I'm not a possession!"

"That's not what Lord Worthless told us," the mover replied. Accepting the truth of this, the maid drooped over the mover's back, arms hanging limply, and allowed herself to be carried out.

Richie and Richina Sterling strolled in, glancing around dispassionately. "I told you this would happen," Richie said to his sister. "I'm sure we could buy the place for a song but, frankly . . . who would want it?"

"The tennis court is nice," Richina pointed out.

"That was built with our money," Richie reminded her. "So that's already ours."

"So it is!" Richina said with a jaunty laugh. As she threw her head back to chortle, her earrings ring and her many bracelets tinkling like a crystal chandelier falling from the ceiling.

Oh, wait, that *had been* a crystal chandelier falling from the ceiling.

"Sell it! Sell it!" Lord Worthless shouted, pointing at the fallen chandelier. "Everything must go," he said to the moving men, who dashed here and there, picking up everything that they could find to sell at the auction.

Doodles Worthless trailed in, dressed in her mother's too-big gown and heeled shoes that are three sizes too large for her. On her head was an elaborate feathered hat that is so big it falls below her eyes. "Richina, look, I'm a big girl like you now. Let's be friends."

"I don't think so, Doodles," Richina answered.

"Not now. Go play with the children."

"But I'm all grown-up. I'm a big girl now," Doodles objected.

"Wearing adult clothing doesn't mean you're a woman," Richina insisted.

Doodles pouted and stamped her foot petulantly. "But I am a big Worthless."

"Perhaps the biggest of them all," Richina quipped drolly.

Snobby Worthless rushed in and threw herself on Richie Sterling, draping herself around his shoulders. "Daw-ling," she cooed. "Let me count your money—oops—I meant let me call you honey."

Richie threw her off. "Let me go, you greedy tart. I know you're only toying with my affections to get your hands on my fortune. You just want the diamonds."

"Diamonds!" Lady Worthless chirped as her thumb pops out of her mouth. "Did someone say diamonds?"

"Dia-mods?" said the baby from atop her head, speaking his first word ever.

"Mother, this wretched boy won't give me his diamond fortune," Snobby complained to Lady Worthless. "I batted my eyelashes and everything, just like you told me to. He's mean! Mean! Mean!" Snobby went to her mother for comfort but Lady Worthless shoved her out of the way as she rushed up to Richie Sterling with the baby still sitting on her head.

"Mr. Sterling, I hear you're not interested in my daughter, Snobby," said Lady Worthless.

"That's right. Not interested at all."

"I quite understand," Lady Worthless agreed. "You should get to know my younger daughter, Doodles, better." Searching around, Lady Worthless tried to find Doodles, but couldn't. "Oh, dear! Oh, dear! Doodles must have blended into the tapestry."

The baby on Lady Worthless's head started to cry once more. "It upsets him when Doodles disappears like that," Lady Worthless explained. The baby slid from her back, pulling off her wig and revealing snow-white hair beneath. "Come back with my hair, you naughty child," Lady Worthless shouted as the baby crawled away, pulling the wig behind him. "Oh, I am much too old for this," she muttered as she trails after him.

Richina Sterling looked at the escaping baby. "Why don't you get a young nanny like everyone else has?" she asks.

"I had one, but Lord Worthless sold her off to help raise money to save the estate," Lady Worthless explained wistfully. "We had better not stand here for too long or we'll be sold too." But her remark came too late, for as she stands there talking, one of the movers scooped her up to carry her off.

"Lord Worthless, help!" Lady Worthless implored her husband for help. "Make this man release me! Tell him I am not for sale!"

"Of course you are for sale, darling," Lord Worthless insisted. "You've been trying to sell our daughters for months now. Why shouldn't I sell you, though I don't know who would want an aged mother like you."

"You beast!" Lady Worthless shouted as the mover carries her away.

Abby Grahame

"Sell! Sell!" Lord Worthless shouted. "Everything must go! I need the money."

Soon the movers had carried out everything. Richie and Richina were left in an empty foyer. "What's the sense in selling everything to save the manor if the manor is unlivable because it's empty?" Richina questioned.

"Who knows?" Richie answered. "And, frankly, who cares? Can I interest you in a game of tennis?"

"That sounds smashing," she agreed and followed him out, her many bracelets making a loud racket as she goes.

For a moment there was silence in the empty room, but then a small voice sounded. "Hello? Where is everybody?" Doodles emerged from the wall, still dressed in her oversized clothing. She blew away a feather from her hat, which had flopped over her woebegone face as she searched the place, wondering where everyone had gone. Finally she heard a pathetic moan from under the table and spied Snobby's shoes peaking out.

Grabbing hold of her sister's feet, Doodles pulled Snobby out from beneath the table. Snobby came to consciousness once more. "I must have fainted," she declared. "Imagine that Richie Sterling not wanting to marry me."

"Or me," Doodles added.

Snobby stood, took Doodles by the hand, and led her to the massive front door, pulling it wide open. "Come along, Doodles," she said bravely. "We'll find some fabulously wealthy men to marry us and buy us fancy things. After all . . . we're Worthless."

Abby Grahame

Chapter Twelve

NORA, FIND ME A DAY DRESS WITH A NICE wide skirt, will you? Something that won't drag on the dirt," Maggie instructed. These Indian summer days were still beautiful and it would be nice to get out on the grounds for a walk. It might be just the thing to help her shake this feeling of being a caged bird.

"How about this, Miss?" Nora suggested, presenting her with a tea-length dress of a simple blue broadcloth with a white collar.

"Perfect," Maggie pronounced, "and I'll need my most comfortable boots. The black ones with the low heels and the hook sides are probably best."

Within minutes Maggie was dressed and Nora had

assisted her in weaving her hair into a French braid fastened with a bow at the back of her neck, letting the rest of her dark curls fall free. "Enjoy your stroll," Nora bid her as Maggie disappeared into the hall.

On the way downstairs Maggie ducked into the dining room, relieved that no one had risen for breakfast yet, although the buffet and the table settings had been laid out. This enabled her to escape with a raisin scone wrapped in a linen napkin without getting bogged down in conversation. As she made her way out a back entrance not far from the stable, the cool snap in the air struck her with new energy. This solo walk was just the thing to clear her head and today was picture-perfect.

As Maggie crossed the rolling green lawn, noticing that the first reds and oranges of the coming fall were already settling in on the trees of the woods ahead of her, she noticed two figures on a path cutting diagonally across the lawn to her right. It took only another second for her to see that it was Therese pushing the baby's carriage. And Michael was strolling alongside them! They saw her but pretended they hadn't. Maggie was certain that they'd deliberately turned their heads away.

Maggie felt as if she'd been stabbed straight through her heart. Without a moment's thought, she headed purposefully toward them. How long had this flirtation between Therese and Michael been going on? And was that Therese insane? Why would she bring James outside on a chilly morning like this? She needed to get that baby inside.

"*Bonjour*, Miss Maggie," Therese greeted her when Maggie came near. "How are you this—"

"What are you thinking?" Maggie demanded, growing red-faced with fury. "Look at the flimsy covering you have over the baby. He's sure to catch a chill."

A blush rose on Therese's cheeks, as well. "I think he is well covered," she defended herself.

"The little guy looks happy enough to me," Michael put in.

"Don't you dare," Maggie muttered, shooting him a withering glare. "You have no opinion about this."

Michael looked as if he were about to say something else, but Maggie's scathing glare made certain he would from there on hold his tongue. Turning her attention back to Therese, Maggie pointed angrily to Wentworth Hall.

"Bring him inside this minute," she commanded. "And from now on you ask permission before you ever bring him outside in inclement weather again. Is that understood?"

"Yes, mademoiselle," Therese agreed, head cast down. She gazed at Michael apologetically and he returned a small smile of understanding.

"Go!" Maggie shouted at Therese.

As the nanny scurried off, Maggie stood there, hands on hips, panting with anger. When she turned to Michael, he was studying her intently. "Inclement weather?" he questioned with a note of sarcasm, spreading his arms wide to indicate the beauty of the blue sky and green rolling hills.

"It's cold," Maggie snapped at him. "And James is just a baby."

"It's not cold, Maggie," Michael disagreed levelly. "What was all that about?"

Maggie studied Michael's handsome face. Her anger was gone, but she had a million questions. Some too dangerous to broach. She settled on asking about Therese. "Why were you walking with Therese?"

"My work is done for the morning and Therese is

pleasant company," Michael explained. "Mrs. Howard suggested I get to know her better."

"Mrs. Howard did?" Maggie questioned, her voice rising once more. "Maybe Mrs. Howard should mind her own business."

"Why shouldn't Mrs. Howard do a little match-making? I'm not too low on the social ladder for a girl like Therese. What's it to you?"

The rush of tears that came into Maggie's eyes took her by surprise and she jammed the heels of her hands into her eyes in a vain attempt to stem the flood.

"Aw, Maggie!" Michael moved toward her but froze. "I didn't mean that. I want to take you in my arms, but I can't. We don't know who might be watching from the house. I'm sorry. I was being horrible to you. Forgive me."

Taking her hands from her eyes, Maggie gazed at him through wet eyes. "What's the sense in pretending, Michael? You must know I still love you and I couldn't stand seeing you with that girl and James." She glanced toward the many windows of Wentworth Hall and knew he was right. As much as she longed to be in his arms, he was right. It wouldn't be wise.

"First time I've seen little Lord Darlington," Michael responded, trying to lighten the mood. "Handsome fellow, no wonder your mother keeps him cloistered up in that nursery. Real lady-killer in the making."

"Yes." Maggie smiled faintly. "He's safe there. In the nursery." They both fell into silence, and Maggie stared off into the fields.

"What are you thinking?" he asked.

"I'm wishing that the rest of the world would just go away and let us be. Why do the opinions of other people have to matter?" she said.

"I don't know why, but somehow they do," Michael replied in a voice filled with pain. "You're not just a regular person, you're a Darlington and that makes it impossible for us. I won't ask you to give up everything you were born to. Not again, at least."

"I don't care about those things," Maggie said, and as the words came out of her mouth she knew they were true. What was wealth if she couldn't have Michael?

"But you still won't run away with me. Because being a Darlington is not only about things. It's family, too," Michael reminded her. "You told me yourself, nothing

Abby Graheme

means more to the Darlingtons than keeping the family lineage and prestige. If you married a groom—you'd never see Wesley or Lila or your parents again. Not to mention, you'd never be allowed to step foot in Wentworth Hall."

"Damn Wentworth Hall!" Maggie cried heatedly. "It's musty and cold, drafty and it's falling apart."

"It's belonged to your family for nearly three centuries." Michael said tenderly. "Wentworth Hall is in your blood."

"A gilded cage is still a cage." Hanging her head, Maggie let her tears fall freely. "I hate what's happened to us, Michael," she whimpered pitifully.

"I know, love," Michael said. The warmth in his voice was like a caress and Maggie let it wrap around her soothingly. What heaven it would be to lean her head on his chest and let him stroke her hair. She ached for his warm touch and the comfort of him. "I wish we could go back to being children and stop time there," she told Michael. "At least then I could keep you near me always."

"I wish it too," Michael agreed, daring to step closer to her. "But it can never be."

* * *

Lila gazed at Teddy Fitzhugh from behind the playing cards fanned out in her hands. He had finally tired of Maggie, and now deigned to pay Lila some attention. He had even taught her to play bezique, a card game he'd learned while on holiday in Italy a few years before. The amazing thing was, while he was still undeniably handsome, he failed to inspire the same feelings he once did in her. Was she really so fickle? This love business was certainly puzzling.

"Lila, it's your turn," Teddy reminded her.

"Oh!" Lila answered, plopping down an ace.

"It's nice to see you two having fun," Lady Darlington said as she walked into the parlor. She nooded hello to Jessica, who was scribbling away in her journal in the corner of the room.

"Yes, Teddy has taught me the most diverting game," Lila said. Though secretly she was a bit bored. "Would you like to take over my hand, Mother? I think I'd like to take a nap before supper."

"If Teddy doesn't mind, I'd love to," her mother answered.

"I don't mind in the least, Lady Darlington," Teddy answered smoothly.

Lila realized that in the past it might have bothered her that Teddy didn't seem to mind her absence. Now she was glad of it. Lila headed upstairs for her "nap," but ran into Nora, who was busily plumping the cushions in one of the guest rooms.

"Nora," Lila said, "just the girl I wanted to see." Maybe Nora would have some insight into why her feelings for Teddy had simply disappeared.

Nora continued plumping the cushions, seemingly lost in thought.

"Nora?" Lila said again. "Noraaa!"

"Oh! Miss Lila." Nora put the cushion down, momentarily flustered. "I didn't hear you."

"You're very distracted today, Nora," Lila observed. "Is something on your mind?"

"Well, now that you mention it, yes, there is." She walked over to the bed and began fixing the pillows.

"You can't just say that without telling me what's distracting you!" Lila exclaimed after several more minutes had passed in silence.

"I didn't want to burden you with it is all," Nora replied as she continued her duties.

"Burden me with what? For Heaven's sake, Nora, come out with it!"

Nora hesitated before replying. Lila wondered if Nora had discovered the same secret she had—about Michael and Maggie. Part of her hoped so, she was dying to talk to *someone* about it, but knew she could never reveal it to anyone herself. It could ruin Maggie forever.

"It's just that I'm worried about my job here at the estate," Nora admitted.

"Why would you worry about that?" Lila asked, genuinely surprised. Nora had grown up at Wentworth Hall. Lila couldn't imagine the place without her.

Nora sighed heavily and turned to face Lila. "I shouldn't tell you this and I wouldn't want to get Therese in trouble."

"Tell me!" Lila implored. Though she wasn't sure she really wanted to hear. After learning about Maggie and Michael, Lila had enough trouble to think about. Lila felt pangs of guilt for judging Maggie so harshly. What she'd taken for coldness was all a mask for the suffering and loneliness she had to be feeling. What a curse to be hopelessly in love with someone she could never have all because of an accident of birth.

Abby Grahame

"All right, since you insist, I'll tell you." Nora's voice brought Lila back to the conversation at hand. "Therese found a letter from your father's lawyer in London and it seemed to mean that your father is selling off pieces of the estate. That means that things must be pretty bad around here. If they're that bad, I could get the sack any day now."

Lila felt her heart drop, alarmed by Nora's words. Could their finances really be that dire? "Are you sure Therese really found a letter like that?"

Nora reached into her apron pocket and produced a letter addressed to the family solicitor. "She gave it to me."

Lila took the letter and quickly perused it. "I'll get to the bottom of this," Lila told Nora as she strode toward the door. "Wait right here."

"Don't say it was me who showed you the letter," Nora requested. "Or Therese either."

"I won't," Lila promised. Her father couldn't sell off Wentworth Hall piece by piece. What was he thinking? It couldn't be true. And if there were rumors flying around that he was doing this, it was almost as bad. Their reputations would be ruined.

Lila knew she'd find her father in his study on the fifth floor of the west wing at this time of day and headed straight to it. Rapping on his door, she didn't wait to be admitted but walked right in. "Father, is it true that you're selling off pieces of the estate?"

"Where did you hear such a thing?" Lord Darlington asked, looking up from the financial ledger book he'd been poring over.

Lila hesitated, not prepared with an answer. "I can't say. But I heard it."

Her father caught her in a concerned stare. Neither of them spoke. Lila was at a loss for what to say next and guessed that her father was also considering what to say before saying it.

"It's not true," Lord Darlington said at last.

She showed him the letter Nora had given her. "I found this," she fibbed. "If it isn't so, what does this mean?"

Lord Darlington glanced at the letter. "I can't imagine you found that letter lying about the house. We will have to have a talk about you being too old to be snooping around my study playing whatever silly game girls your age play. In the meantime, let me put your fears to rest. I wanted our solicitor to handle an insurance reevaluation for me. I requested that he get some up-to-date prices on our art and parts of our property so that our insurance would reflect the current replacement value."

Lila's shoulders sagged with relief. "I knew it couldn't be," she gushed. "I just had to hear it from you."

"You needn't worry, Lila. The Darlingtons may not enjoy the wealth of yesterday, but we are far from destitute."

Fighting the impulse to throw her arms around her father, a familiarity that always made him uneasy, Lila smiled at Lord Darlington. "Thank you for being frank with me, Father," she said. "I was so concerned."

"Don't think about it for another moment," Lord Darlington said. "Now, if you will leave me to double-check these estate expenditures."

"Of course."

Lila hurried back to her bedroom to give Nora the good news. "It's all fine. It's all something or other about having proper insurance. There's no cause to worry."

"That's wonderful," Nora said happily. "Thank you for finding out, Miss Lila." As Nora crossed to the desk near the window to pick up the soiled laundry, she looked out. "Did you know your brother was coming home?"

Lila ran to the window to see for herself. A slim, handsome young man with blond hair so like the pale shade of their mother's had emerged from the passenger side of a shiny motorcar with large, narrow white tires and no roof. The driver was a young man of the same age, a little shorter than Teddy but still quite tall. His honey-blond hair caught the sunlight and made him look quite dashing. She wouldn't call him handsome, exactly. He wasn't polished like Teddy or even Wes. But what was really remarkable was his laugh. She could hear it even from here! Lila liked this fellow instantly.

Wesley had spent the early part of the summer in the United States with his American friend Ian who was also studying in Oxford. The driver must be Ian. She'd assumed Wesley was going directly back to school from America but was delighted that he hadn't.

Not wasting another moment by the window, Lila bounded out of the room and ran all the way down to the first floor. She encountered Wesley and his friend as they were coming in the front door, suitcases in hand.

Abby Grahame

"Wes!" she greeted him with a happy shout. "Do Father and Mother expect you? They didn't tell me you were coming."

Wesley set his suitcase down and hugged her warmly. "Look at you!" he cried, taking her by the shoulders and studying her. "All grown up since I last saw you. You look smashing, Lila!"

Lila felt herself blush as she basked in the warmth of his praise. Wesley turned to his friend. "Ian, this is my little sis I've been telling you about, only she's looking a lot older than the last time she and I were together."

Ian stepped forward and extended his hand. Somehow Lila knew he meant to shake rather than kiss her hand and she pumped it enthusiastically. "Ian Martin," he introduced himself. "Glad to meet you, Lila."

"Glad to meet you," Lila echoed, grinning. His hand was warm and strong and he had a pleasant, open face.

"Is Maggie around?"

"I think she went out for a walk."

"Where are Mother and Father?" Wesley asked.

"Father's in his study and Mother is in the parlor with our houseguests, the Fitzhughs."

"Set your suitcase down, Ian. The butler will get it," Wesley said.

Ian gazed around the foyer, clearly awed by it. "Better stick close to me, you two. I could get lost in a place this gigantic."

"Your place in Newport was this big," Wesley said.

"Not by half," Ian disagreed. "This is a palace."

Percival the head butler greeted them and Wesley requested that the rest of Ian's and his luggage be brought in. "You can put Mr. Martin's things in the guest bedroom next to mine," he instructed.

"Very good, sir." In minutes Percival enlisted two butlers to bring in the rest of the bags. Percival himself carried several issues of a newspaper. "These were on the floor of the car, sir. What would you like me to do with them?"

"Thanks, Percival," Wesley said. "I'll take those."

"Why are you keeping those old papers?" Lila asked.

"They're part of the reason I came home. I want to talk to Father about them. See for yourself." Wesley took the top paper and set the rest of them at his feet. Quickly flipping through it, he soon found what he'd been searching for and handed the open paper to Lila.

Not sure what she was looking at, Lila began to read aloud. "The Worthless Saga," she said. "This sounds funny." But as she scanned the article, her eyes widened with horror. "Wes, this is about us!"

"I think that's a pretty safe guess," Wesley agreed.

Lila's head was reeling with disbelief. Was she the character they called Doodles? She had to be! Constantly overlooked, forgotten about! How completely humiliating! How mortifying! This was horrible!

"Who could have written this?" Lila asked.

"I have no idea," Wesley replied. "But one thing is clear enough: The author of this is someone living here at Wentworth Hall."

Chapter Thirteen

THERESE STOOD BY THE KITCHEN WINDOW watching Michael and Maggie talking out on the path. Was Maggie crying? From this distance it was hard to tell. Therese was the one who should be crying after the way Maggie had spoken to her that morning. She didn't feel like crying though. Instead, she was more curious to see what was going on outside.

Today's walk had confirmed the suspicions that had been forming in her mind from the first moment she laid eyes on Michael. Seeing him up close and then experiencing Maggie's rage at the sight of him with the baby and Therese had cast away all doubts. What she suspected was true. It seemed every generation of Darlington had secrets to answer for.

Couldn't Michael see it? Was it her duty as his friend to point it out? It didn't seem fair that the upper classes could keep secrets to protect themselves, regardless of how it hurt other people. She knew all too well the pain of that.

"Therese," Mrs. Howard's voice cut through her reverie. "Where is James?"

"He is in his crib, Madame," Therese answered. "He naps at this hour. I thought to slip away for a moment or two."

"Good, then join us upstairs in the dining room," Mrs. Howard commanded. "I need to address the entire staff."

"*Oui*, Madame." Therese reluctantly left the window and followed the head housekeeper up the servants' staircase to the dining room where the rest of the servants were already assembled.

Therese stood alongside Nora. Scanning the anxious faces around her, Therese wondered if some of them were about to be fired. It could be a hundred other things, of course, but that was what was on each of their minds. She could see it in the darting eyes and bitten lips of her coworkers.

Mrs. Howard held a newspaper over her head. It was the *Sussex Courier*. "As some of you may already know," she began, "Master Wesley has just returned home. On his journey back to Sussex, he came across a newspaper publishing thinly disguised satires about the Darlington Family."

Mrs. Howard put down the paper and waited until the buzz of shocked murmurs had subsided. "Master Wesley believes that this embarrassment to the Darlingtons contains information that could only be gleaned by someone living at Wentworth Hall. And since it targets the family, it is most probably a member of the serving staff."

"Do you really think it could be one of us?" Grace asked, personally affronted.

"I think there's a distinct possibility," Mrs. Howard confirmed, anger flashing in her eyes. "And if that is so, I find it very sad indeed. The Darlingtons have always treated the staff here at Wentworth Hall with the utmost respect and consideration. If any one of you has been so ungrateful as to . . ."

Mrs. Howard's remaining words were lost as once more the din of excited speculation filled the room. "Quiet! Quiet, please," Mrs. Howard insisted. "This would be an opportune moment for the author of these satires to confess."

Therese waited along with the rest of the staff for

someone to speak up. The truth was, it could have been any of them. She'd heard any number of the maids making fun of the Darlingtons. She herself had laughed along.

Minutes passed but no one stepped forward. When next Mrs. Howard spoke, she kept her gaze on Therese. "If no one admits to this egregious breach of privacy, we may all lose our jobs. Do you really think the Darlingtons will tolerate being made laughingstocks by someone in their own household?"

Others on the staff noticed that Therese was being singled out and turned toward her. Therese could feel the burn of embarrassment flushing her cheeks. "I do not know who did this, but it was most certainly not me," she felt compelled to defend herself. "For one thing, I have never learned to write in English."

"If you ask me," Nora spoke up, "that Jessica Fitzhugh is a likely suspect. She's always making disparaging remarks about the Darlingtons, as if she thinks she's too good for them."

"Miss Fitzhugh is one of those lampooned in the satires," Mrs. Howard pointed out.

"I've read them," Nora argued. "I saw the paper on

Lady Darlington's vanity and couldn't help but glance at it since it was very clear that whatever it was had upset her ladyship; and if you ask me, Jessica Fitzhugh—and Teddy Fitzhugh, for that matter—get off very lightly. Nothing is mocked about him, and the worst thing that's said of Jessica is that she wears too much jewelry. She probably stuck that in there just so she wouldn't look guilty."

"She is always writing in that funny red notebook," Helen put in.

"And it must be hard to write with her nose up in the air like that all the time," added Grace.

"But why would she do such a thing?" Rose protested. "She has no need for the money."

"Maybe she's jealous," Nora suggested.

"She'll soon have much more money than the Darlingtons," Rose said. "Why should she be jealous of them?"

"Maybe because the Darlingtons are a family and all she has is that aggravating brother of hers, Teddy," Nora argued.

"She doesn't seem to think he's annoying," Grace pointed out. "Those twins dote on each other."

"There is no sense indulging in idle and pointless

Abby Grahame

speculation," Mrs. Howard spoke loudly. "Whoever is responsible for this will confess within the week or it is my firm belief that the Darlingtons will do the only thing they can do—replace the entire staff. You are dismissed. Please return promptly to your duties."

Despite Mrs. Howard urging that they get back to work, the staff milled about in the dining room discussing the newspaper satires. "No one is getting the sack over this," Nora told Grace, Helen, and Therese with confidence. "Who are they going to replace us with? How many others are willing to work for little more than room and board like we get here? Not many, I can tell you that."

"But that's all the more reason why a person might want to make extra money on the side by selling a funny story to a newspaper," Therese pointed out.

"There are other ways to make extra besides embarrassing the Darlingtons," Nora objected.

Mrs. Howard came by, clapping her hands sharply. "Back to work, all of you."

"Yes, ma'am," Helen spoke for all of them.

As they dispersed Therese came alongside Nora. "Selling articles might get you your tearoom faster," she said.

Nora whirled on her, clearly offended. "I told you. I take in sewing," she said, speaking in a confidential whisper. "Are you accusing me?"

"I am not accusing anyone," Therese insisted.

"Well I don't believe you can't write in English. You can certainly read it," Nora said, giving Therese a pointed look.

The solicitor's letter. "Reading and writing are not the same," Therese said.

"Hmm," Nora replied. "And how did you learn English in France, anyway?"

"My mother taught me. She lived in England for a time," Therese said. "Think, dear Nora, it wasn't me. I have nowhere to go. Why would I risk a warm bed and food in my stomach for a few pounds?"

"I still say it's that Jessica," Nora muttered as they headed out of the room.

"You will lose your position for certain if you wrongly accuse one of the Fitzhughs," Therese pointed out.

"You're right," Nora agreed. "But I might just plant the idea in Lila's head."

"How would you do that?" Therese asked.

"I have my ways," Nora said with assurance.

Chapter Fourteen

THE SUSSEX COURIER

THE FURTHER ADVENTURES OF . . .
THE WORTHLESS SAGA

Another rib-tickling installment of our
popular ongoing new series
"Wild Stallions in the Ballroom"

What was the scene like at a recent country
dance attended by those ever-entertaining
Worthless sisters? Our spies tell us it was
quite the crush!

Doodles and Snobby Worthless stood in the ballroom of their dilapidated and now empty estate, Faded Glory Manor. They concocted ball gowns by ripping down the peeling wallpaper and folding them into dresses. "It doesn't matter that Father has sold all our possessions, Doodles," Snobby told her sister. "By throwing this ball we will find husbands with fabulous fortunes. They will heap jewels on us and restore Faded Glory Manor to its former grandeur."

"Who has been invited?" asked Doodles.

"All our friends and neighbors! Here are some of our friends now," Snobby cried. "Welcome, neighbors. Do come in."

A troop of local shepherds in muddy boots marched in. "Thanks for the invite. Where's the grub?" says one.

Abby Graham

"Grub?" Snobby inquired, confused.

"The food we were promised," another farmer reminded her.

"Oh, that," Snobby simpered. "It's on its way."

"It better come soon," another farmer grumbled.

Snobby caught sight of a more suitable guest coming into the ballroom and hurried toward him. "It's Duke Oldenfat," she trilled with delight.

The duke, who is a hundred if he's a day, grinned and winked at Snobby. "So nice of you to invite me, my dear. You know how I've admired you from afar."

"Not that far," Snobby reminded him. "You

sit under my window and recite bawdy limericks."

"Ah, yes. You once inspired me," the duke agreed. He squared his shoulders as he prepared to recite. "There was a young woman from Dorset who would let me remove her—"

"That will be enough of that," Snobby interrupted.

"Hey, where's the food?" yelled one of the farmers.

"Coming," Snobby told him. "Doodles, dear, would you go see if you can scrap up something to eat around here," Snobby requested. When Doodles didn't answer, Snobby realized that with her sister's propensity for blending into the background she would never find her now that she'd been literally dressed in wallpaper.

Abby Grahame

"Food!" another farmer shouted. "You promised us food!"

"Put a sock in it!" Snobby bellowed back. Turning back to Duke Oldenfat she smiled graciously because she knew that he could be an excellent source of funding and at his age wouldn't last long. Snobby dreams of the day when she would be a Merry Widow.

"Did you like the poem?" Duke Oldenfat asked, drool spilling from his lips as he looked at Snobby with unabashed lechery.

"Utterly divine," Snobby crooned. Wanting to hurry things along, she took the sides of her dress and yanked them suggestively down so her skinny shoulders were exposed. "Here, duke, sniff me for a while," she said leaning close to the old duke. "Tell me if you like my perfume."

The duke held his nose.

"You don't love it?" Snobby asked, aghast.

"Frankly my dear, everything about you has started to stink. How long do you think you can toy with my affections? You're young enough to be my daughter and I no longer think it would be fun to have a spoiled brat running around my lavish estate." He bowed deeply, and the effort he expended brought on a coughing fit.

"But Duke, I could tend to you in your dotage," Snobby insisted, solicitously helping him stand straight.

"Sorry, young lady. I retract my offer. I bid you adieu." The duke stormed off, leaving Snobby there to watch him leave. "Oh, who cares about you, you old coot?!" she shouted after him. "I still have Richard, who adores me, and he's richer than you."

Abby Grahame

"Did you say I adore you?"

Snobby whirls around to see Richard behind her. "Of course you do," Snobby replied with confidence. "Time is running short. When shall we marry?"

"To be honest, Snobby, time is not running short," Richard replied.

"It's not?" Snobby questioned.

"No. It's run out."

"Run out?!" Snobby cried, shocked. "What do you mean? You adore me!"

"Alas, once I did. But now I have my inheritance and I see that . . . well, that . . ." Richard hesitated, momentarily at a loss for words. "There's no other way to say it, Snobby: I'm just too good for you."

Lord Worthless enters, dragging a chandelier behind him. "Who is too good?" he inquired.

"Daddy, Richard thinks he's too good for me now that he is fabulously wealthy," Snobby explained, running to her father's side.

"Well, of course he is," Lord Worthless confirmed. "Everyone is too good for us these days."

"Who will I marry, then, Daddy?" Snobby whined.

Doodles Worthless came in at that moment. "Why don't you marry your secret admirer?" she asked guilelessly.

"Who?" asked Lord Worthless.

"Shhh!!!!" Snobby hissed at Doodles.

Abby Grahame

"Oh, is it a real secret?" Doodles asked, covering her mouth with her hand.

"Who is this secret admirer?" Lord Worthless asked Snobby. "Does he have money?"

"There is no such person," Snobby told him. "You know how Doodles is."

"Do I?" Lord Worthless pondered. "She's always disappearing like that. Most confusing." He turned to Richard and held up the chandelier. "Care to buy a lighting fixture?" he asked. "It literally fell right into my hands."

"Do you mean it fell from the ceiling?" Richard inquired.

"Yes!" Lord Worthless confirmed. "It keeps happening to me. I suddenly discover that I'm holding a doorknob or a kitchen cabinet handle. Chandeliers fall right into my arms.

Wall moldings fall into my pockets. I seem to have become a magnet for all sorts of pieces of the estate crashing down around me. It's most perplexing!"

"Perhaps your estate could use some fixing up," Richard suggested delicately.

"Faded Glory Manor?! Never! Faded Glory Manor has stood just as it is for over three hundred years. If I did anything to change it, it would no longer be, well . . . Worthless."

"Exactly," Richard agreed.

"Precisely," Lord Worthless said. Nodding, he surveyed his crumbling estate, confident that it would always be Worthless . . . as it should be.

Abby Grahame

MAGGIE HAD NEVER SEEN HER FATHER IN such a state. His skin was red as a beet and the veins at his temple throbbed visibly. The *Sussex Courier* was spread on the desk in front of him. He had called the entire family to his study to "discuss" the satires Wesley had brought to their attention. At the moment, though, he was so infuriated that he was incapable of anything resembling discussion. Standing beside her husband, the usually mild-mannered Lady Darlington appeared equally put out, her arms folded tightly across her chest.

"Is there any truth here, Maggie?" she blasted their oldest daughter. "Have you offended both Teddy and the duke?"

"No! I've told you ten times! No!"

"There had better not be anything to this," Lord Darlington muttered darkly, holding Maggie in his scrutinizing glare.

"I have told you how I feel about your getting married soon," Lady Darlington said in a low, angry tone. "The older you get, the more difficult it will be for you. We have presented you with two highly suitable candidates for husbands and it seems, according to this, that you have alienated and rebuffed them both."

"You both know this is all lies," Lila jumped to Maggie's defense. "These satires show you not caring for the estate. Is that true? Of course not! And it portrays the duke's ball to have taken place here—which we all know isn't true. Are we even certain this is about us? Perhaps we're leaping to conclusions."

"Please, Lila," Wesley said, putting his arm protectively around her shoulders. "It's pretty obvious. This is us, without a doubt."

"Well, just because we realize it doesn't mean everyone will know it's our family being skewered," Lord Darlington allowed. "No one around here pays much

Abby Grahame

attention to this cheap rag. Anyone who matters reads *The London Times*."

"Well, that's true," Lady Darlington agreed, seeming to calm down a bit.

"We had better hope so, at least until we can find out who is behind this scurrilous tripe and put a stop to it," Lord Darlington said, his anger rising again. "And when I find out who it is that person will be sorry he or she was ever born."

Lord Darlington dismissed them all, with a reminder to be careful who they trust. Maggie followed the rest of the family out into the hallway. Noticing that Lila appeared on the verge of tears, Maggie put her hand on her sister's shoulder. "It's not as bad as all that," she soothed. "Try to think of it as funny."

"Funny!" Lila shouted. "They depict me as fading into the wallpaper and eating moths! They make me out to be an imbecile!" As tears splashed down her cheeks, Lila fled down the hallway.

"Poor kid," Wesley sympathized.

"Go! See what you can do," Lady Darlington urged her son. "You've always known how to cheer her up."

"I'll try," Wesley agreed, hurrying after Lila.

"It will be all right, Mother," Maggie said, desperate to say anything that might take the stricken expression from her mother's face.

Lady Darlington forced an insincere smile. "Honestly, dear, could it be any worse?" The parallel frown lines between her eyebrows had never looked deeper. "I want to go look in on James. Would you like to come along?"

"No. Well not today," Maggie declined. Her mother gave her a pointed look as if to say *You can't avoid him forever*, but she accepted her answer. Maggie retreated down the hall. She headed for the staircase, and met Teddy coming up, holding the latest *Sussex Courier*. "Where did you get that?" she demanded.

"Where do you think? The newsstand in town." The smug way he was grinning at her was infuriating and it told Maggie that he was well aware of the paper's spurious contents. If she could have wiped the grin off his face with a slap, she would have gladly done so. Instead, she chose to ice him out without a glance as they passed on the stairs.

"It's a hoot, isn't it, Snobby?" he hissed as their shoulders brushed.

"I wouldn't laugh, Richie Sterling," she shot back.

"Why shouldn't I? Richie and Richina come off looking pretty good compared to the rest."

Maggie knew he was goading her and that the best thing to do would be to keep going, but she felt helpless to resist. "Funny, isn't it, that you and Jessica get such light treatment?" she challenged. "One might even think that you and your sister are the authors of this trash."

"Oh, please," Teddy scoffed. "Neither Jessica nor I have any need for the pittance the rag would pay for this bit of entertainment. And I have better things to do with my time than think about you and your absurd family."

"Absurd?!" Maggie fumed, immediately regretting that she'd registered the jab at all.

"Completely absurd," Teddy twisted the knife. "Your family is exactly as depicted in this paper and everyone will recognize it immediately."

"You ingrate!" Maggie growled. "And after my parents took you in."

"Don't insult my intelligence," he came back at her fiercely. "You know your father simply wanted to get a piece of our fortune by selling you off to me. To think I almost fell for it too. I will always consider not marrying you was a bullet dodged."

"As will I," Maggie said.

"I don't look so bad to you now that you realize what your choices are, though, do I?" Teddy added with a smarmy smile. "You passed on a young, handsome millionaire in favor of a thousand-year-old duke. Good work, Maggie. That was really using your brain. What a fool!"

It took every ounce of Maggie's self-control not to leap at him and rake his face with her nails. He was the most arrogant, conceited person she'd ever met. "I can't wait until you leave here," she spat.

"Neither can I," Teddy shot back. "It won't be long now, either. I turn eighteen next month and then the family fortune will be mine. Jessica and I will be gone the next day; You can count on that. The only reason we came in the first place was to cull some social standing from the Darlington name. What a mistake that turned out to be. After these satires make the rounds, your precious family name will be so irrevocably tarnished you'll want to change it."

* * *

"Breathe, Lila, please!" Ian crouched in front of the straight-back floral damask couch where Lila sat sobbing and hyperventilating. "You're going to pass out."

Lila's hands were pressed against her collarbone as her chest heaved up and down. "I-I-I-I," was all she could manage to say. These newspaper satires were so awful! Her coming out into society was only a year and some months away, and now it was ruined. She was a laughingstock. Who would want to be seen at her ball? What young man would ever ask her out?

Wesley strode into the room. "There you are! I've been searching everywhere for you!"

"I think she's hysterical," Ian explained, answering the unspoken question in Wesley's eyes.

Wesley dropped down onto the couch beside Lila and took hold of her shoulders. "Calm down, Lila! It's not that bad. Really!"

The sound of her big brother's voice filtered through the haze of panic surrounding Lila and gradually her heartbeat slowed and her breathing followed. "That's the girl," she heard him say. Through her tears, his familiar face slowly came into focus. "You're not facing this alone,

Lila. We're all here and we'll get through this together."

Lila gulped in great swallows of air as her tears subsided.

"There might even be a positive side to all this," Wesley added.

With her curiosity piqued, Lila rubbed the tears from her eyes. "A positive side?"

Wesley sat back on the couch and folded his arms. "Well, consider this. Suppose everyone does guess that we're the Worthless family." He stopped to chuckle. "I sort of think the name is amusing."

"Oh, how can you?" Lila scolded.

"Well, maybe not. But anyway, now that it's out in the open that the Darlington fortune isn't what it once was, there's no more reason to pretend. If the need to keep up appearances is gone, then Father might seriously entertain my ideas about modernizing the estate business, selling off what we can."

"Business?" Lila cried, shocked. "This is our home. You're the one who will inherit the place; why would you want it sold?"

"Because we need the money now, Lila," Wesley explained. "The farmers are abandoning our lands to procure

Ably Grahame

jobs in the city. No one wants to do that sort of labor for little more than room and board on our lands when they could make their own salary. And Wentworth Hall depends in large part on the money made from those farms."

"I can't believe it." Lila echoed in disbelief.

"The estate is enormous. Do we honestly need all of this land? And the stables! Do we need all these horses? Mother says Maggie doesn't ride anymore. Motorcars are becoming more and more common these days, and the few who haven't already will soon be switching over, so there's no need for carriage horses anymore."

"You can't let Michael go!" Lila objected.

"Michael's a fine worker. He'll find a position elsewhere. We'll help get him placed if he wants. I could even look into city jobs for him."

Lila shook her head. "Oh, Wes, I don't know."

Wesley put his arm around Lila and handed her his white linen handkerchief. "Wipe your eyes and blow your nose," he suggested. "We're going into the modern world and it's time the Darlingtons caught up with it."

"But what are we going to do about these satires?" Lila asked.

"We're going to ignore them," Wesley replied. "No one else has caught on that they might be about us. Or at least we haven't heard about it."

"They're just silly, really," Ian agreed.

"Easy for you to say. You two aren't in them," Lila pointed out.

"True, but you mustn't let them bother you so much," Wesley insisted. "I'm almost sorry I brought them to everyone's attention."

"You had to," Lila said.

"I suppose I did," Wesley agreed, "but still . . . stiff upper lip and all that."

"It's hard to do," Lila complained.

"This will blow over," Ian said encouragingly.

Lila really looked at him for the first time since he'd arrived. His brown eyes were flecked with specks of green and gold, which was rather striking. He might be shorter than Wes and Teddy, but he had nice broad shoulders. "Do you really think so?" she asked, unconvinced.

"Yes, I do," Ian stated. "And if you don't mind my saying, the satires have it all wrong anyway. Particularly when it comes to you."

"So do you think I seem like the kind of girl who fades into the background?" Lila dared to ask.

"Absolutely not," Ian insisted adamantly. "It's very clear that whoever wrote these ridiculous pieces doesn't know you very well, or even at all."

For the first time in hours Lila smiled gently.

"If you were in America you wouldn't even be bothering about any of this," Ian went on. "In Newport, Rhode Island, where I come from, there are lots of wealthy families with lovely homes who don't have titles and are proud that they made their fortunes on their own. The first of the Astor family, one of the wealthiest in the country, came from Holland and set up shop in New York City as a butcher. The family is proud of it."

"He's right," Wesley agreed.

"But the things they said about me," Lila reminded them.

"If you laugh about it, everyone else will too," Ian insisted. "Besides, no one will recognize the beautiful girl I see from those descriptions."

Lila's teary eyes brightened. "That's nice of you to say."

"It's true!" Ian maintained.

Therese appeared at the doorway, holding the baby.

"Who is this?" Wesley asked under his breath, clearly impressed with Therese's beauty.

"Are you ready for your French lesson, Mademoiselle Lila?" Therese inquired. "I'm about to take James for his nap."

"Right. I forgot all about that. Yes, I'll be there in a few minutes. But first some introductions," Lila said. "Therese, this is my brother Wes, and his friend Ian Martin," Lila made the introduction.

"*Bonjour,*" Therese greeted them, paying special attention to Wesley.

Wesley and Ian stood politely. "Nice to meet you, Therese," Wesley said as he went to her side. "And this must be my baby brother." He looked at James in Therese's arms as she bounced him gently, causing the baby to giggle with delight.

"Look at those green eyes and dark hair. He doesn't look much like the rest of us, does he?" Wesley observed.

"He must take after his father, then," Therese said.

"Father does have dark hair," Lila pointed out. "What's left of it, anyway. Funny how the rest of us went on Mother. All blond hair and brown eyes."

"Yes," Therese demurred. "Funny."

Abby Grahame

THERESE BENT OVER JAMES'S CRIB TO LAY him down for his late afternoon nap. He cooed at her, his little arms and legs windmilling. She rubbed his belly to settle him and sang a French lullaby that named all the French cathedrals in a lilting melody. Finally his green eyes drifted shut and she laid his crocheted blanket over him. Maybe people would expect her to resent little Lord James for being born into a life of privilege. But she felt a kinship with this tiny baby. He, too, had been manipulated like a chess piece. The only difference between them was that he ended up on the right side.

Settling on the mahogany rocking chair beside the crib, she waited to make sure he was truly asleep before leaving the nursery. He was such a beautiful baby, but it was true that he didn't look like the others in his family. How they could not realize whom he did look like was beyond her. The Darlingtons were so wrapped up in themselves it was as if the servants didn't exist.

One glance at Michael had told her the truth, and from then on it had been blazingly obvious to her. His striking, large green eyes were the same eyes baby James had, lucky boy.

Lady Darlington wasn't his mother either. Therese was sure of that. A woman her age having a baby! It strained credibility. It was clear enough that Maggie was the one who loved Michael.

Maggie was James's mother.

Any fool could see it!

And yet . . . No one seemed to be aware of it—not even Michael! During their walk this morning, she kept thinking he would make the connection. It was the reason she had invited him to stroll with her again! She kept waiting and waiting, but it never happened.

Therese had to admit, it was admirable of Lady Darlington to keep the baby. The usual thing would have been for Maggie and her mother to go abroad, have the baby in some convent or home for unwed mothers, and then give the baby up for adoption.

How Maggie must have fought to keep James. It was the only explanation. Yet she was so disinterested in him now. It was probably the only way she could be sure no one would guess. If it came out that she'd had a baby out of wedlock—and the father was the stable groom—she would be ruined. There would be no marrying her off to a duke or anyone else, in that case.

Therese was an illegitimate child herself, so the thought that Maggie had fought for her baby made her warm toward the girl. How different Therese's life would have been if her father had fought to keep her instead of letting her mother raise her alone.

Steps in the hall broke into Therese's thoughts. Nora came to the door, leaning against the doorjamb. "You and I have to have a chat," Nora insisted, and her expression was not friendly.

"Of course," Therese agreed. "You seem upset."

"I'll get right to the point," Nora said. "I believe you are the one writing these awful satires about the Darlingtons."

"Why do you think that?" Therese asked. "I thought you suspected Miss Fitzhugh?"

"I still don't like that snooty Miss Fitzhugh, but it just doesn't make sense that she would go through the trouble. And your trying to pin it on me and my tearoom makes me suspicious of you. I think you came all the way from France hoping that the Darlingtons would offer you a lavish life with hardly any work involved. That hasn't turned out to be the case, and now you're trying to get some fast cash to return to France."

"What about you?" Therese countered. "You told me you have hopes to leave service."

"But I'll earn the money by sewing. You have no other skills to offer."

"I could teach French," Therese argued.

"How would you manage it in your spare time?" Nora insisted. "No, your only chance was to write these wicked satires. You admitted to me that you don't like the Darlingtons."

"Maybe it wasn't nice to say what I said about them, but they haven't been so nice to me, either."

Abbey Grahame

"Why? What have you got against them?" Nora challenged.

"For one thing, Lord Darlington unjustly despises me," Therese spit out. "He wants me sent back to France."

Nora looked suddenly pale. "How do you know that?"

"How do *you* know it?" Therese shot back. It was clear that this news had come as no surprise to Nora.

"I heard them talking."

"So did I," Therese told her. "When Lord Darlington gets agitated, he forgets to keep his voice down. The entire staff probably knows how he feels by now."

"That still doesn't give you the right to destroy good people," Nora said, but her voice was calmer. "I knew from the start you weren't to be trusted," Nora added.

Nora's dart hit its spot in Therese's heart. She liked Nora and didn't want her to think ill of her. "I'm sorry you feel that way," she said sincerely, feeling very misunderstood and more alone than ever. "Just because I don't like the Darlingtons doesn't mean I wrote those satires."

From his crib, James fussed. Getting up, Therese went to the crib and stroked his belly, trying to soothe him back to sleep, but his eyes opened. "Once his eyes open, he's done sleeping," Therese told Nora. "I need to feed him now."

"I should get back to work too," Nora said, ducking out of the room.

"*Oui,*" Therese said, unbuttoning James's romper to check his diaper.

Once she had changed the baby, Therese brought him to his high chair in the empty dining room. She found a dish of warmed peas set on the chair's tray along with James's tiny silver spoon.

Therese sat beside James, feeding him, her mind replaying the events of the day, especially her concerns about whether or not to tell Michael of what she was certain was the truth. She was so lost in thought that when Mrs. Howard spoke to her, she startled, dropping the spoon.

"You were a thousand miles away, weren't you, Therese?" the head housekeeper observed. "I'd advise you to keep your mind on your work, especially when tending to a baby."

"Yes, madame," Therese answered, stooping to retrieve the spoon and cleaning it on a linen napkin. She had to stifle the urge to defend herself, to say that she did her job very well and she was entitled to think her own thoughts while doing so. But what would be the sense in arguing? It would only make Mrs. Howard dislike her even more than she apparently already did.

"I realized the other day while I was addressing the staff why you look so familiar to me," Mrs. Howard said, and her voice was mildly accusing. "I knew your mother."

"You did?" Therese asked. "She worked for Lord Darlington's sister a long time ago."

"Nineteen years ago," Mrs. Howard supplied the exact time frame, her eyes boring into Therese as if searching for something. "That's how old you are, isn't it?"

"*Oui*, Madame," Therese agreed, getting up to wipe mashed peas from James's cheeks. She was glad for the reason to turn away from Mrs. Howard's piercing inspection.

"Why have you come here?" Mrs. Howard demanded sternly.

Therese's heart banged in her chest. All along, she had been afraid this would happen—that someone might make the connection between her and her mother. Just when she'd begun to relax and trust that her secret was safe, it had happened. What was she to do now?

"I don't know what you mean," Therese claimed, lifting James from his chair.

"I believe you do," Mrs. Howard insisted.

Therese faced her and hoped her expression gave away nothing. "No, I do not," she said, working to keep her gaze level and her voice even.

The two women faced each other, their eyes locked in a combative stare. James broke the stalemate with a whimper that forced Therese to turn her attention to his food-covered face. "What a messy boy you are," Therese said with a smile, lifting him from the high chair. "We'd better get you cleaned and changed."

Although Mrs. Howard was still scrutinizing her, Therese pretended not to notice as she left the room with James in her arms. "*Bonjour*, Mrs. Howard," she said in the lightest tone she could muster, as though there were no tension between them.

The tension was real enough, however, she thought as she headed back to the nursery with the baby. It explained the harsh looks Mrs. Howard had been sending her way. When she came to Wentworth Hall, she had worried someone on the staff might recall her mother. Still, it didn't really mean anything. It could just be a coincidence. Couldn't it?

"Hey, there!"

Therese turned and saw Wesley hurrying to catch up to her on the staircase. "How's my new baby brother doing today?" he asked with a bright-eyed smile.

"He's a little messy after his lunch, I'm afraid," Therese answered. "I am on my way to clean him up."

"Might I tag along?" Wesley requested.

"Of course, monsieur," Therese replied. After her encounter with Mrs. Howard, she welcomed his friendly manner.

"Please, call me Wes."

"I could not," she demurred.

"Of course you can—at least when we're alone."

Therese's stomach dropped. Alone? Was he flirting with her? She had the distinct impression that he was. She could never allow that.

"I've never been to France, but I'm dying to see it," Wesley said as he trailed her down the hall toward the nursery. "Are you planning any visits home?"

"I may be going home sooner than I planned," Therese said evasively.

"Why would that be?" Wesley asked.

"I believe I am under suspicion as the author of those terrible articles about your family," she admitted, seeing no harm in being frank.

He grew serious. "They're terrible, aren't they?"

"Maybe no one really reads them," Therese said.

"I think you might be right," Wesley allowed. "At least no one that Mother and Father socialize with. Besides, since I've returned, there haven't been any more printed. I gave the newspaper management a strict talking-to. I hated to use such tactics, but I would do anything to protect my family. And the Darlington name is revered enough to have an effect on people."

"I'm sure," Therese replied, with a hint of bitterness that Wesley did not catch.

In the nursery, she laid James on his bassinet and began unbuttoning his little romper while he cooed. "He's a sweet little guy, isn't he?" Wesley observed, coming alongside Therese.

Wesley was charming. Of course he would be. She imagined his father had been much the same way when he was younger.

Abby Grahame

"I apologize, Monsieur Wesley. Can I ask you to leave me to my work? Your mother will not approve of you being in here with me."

"Oh, she won't mind," Wesley disagreed.

"Please!" Therese insisted with more heat than she had intended. "I am asking you to leave."

Wesley's face clouded over and Therese regretted it. She'd made herself a challenge. And men like the Wesleys and Lord Darlingtons of the world loved nothing more than a challenge.

Wesley backed out of the room, his expression somehow a mask of both slighted dignity and stubborn interest. "Sorry that I've taken up so much of your time," he said.

"Not at all," Therese said politely. The odd thing was, she had the distinct feeling that, under different circumstances, she and Wesley could have been good friends. But the current circumstances were not her doing. And it would serve her well to remember that.

"Swear to me, Nora," Michael demanded, waving the *Sussex Courier* in front of her. "Swear to me that you had nothing to do with this." He tossed the newspaper into the slop bucket next to the horses' stalls to demonstrate his contempt for the paper.

"Michael! How dare you even think it!" Nora replied indignantly, scraping her boot on a stall door to rid it of the droppings she'd accidentally stepped into. "How could you even suspect me of such a thing?"

"I know you're dying for that tearoom you're dreaming about. The newspaper must pay a good deal for this. And you're the only one who knows about Maggie and me."

"I wouldn't know," Nora insisted, pouting. "I'm both hurt and flattered that you think I might be the author."

"Why would you be flattered?" Michael asked.

"They're rather clever."

"Clever!" Michael thundered. "How can you say that? Do you know how disastrous it would be for Maggie and for me if anyone realized there was ever anything between us?"

"Didn't I warn you at the time that you were playing with fire?" Nora came back at him. "I told you to leave that girl alone, but you wouldn't listen. So don't complain to me now that you've gone and had your own way."

"You were right, Nora, I admit it."

"Honestly, you underestimate me. You know how

much I love gossip, but I have never mentioned a thing to a living soul—not about you and Maggie nor about the baby."

"The baby? What does Lord James have to do with any of this?"

Nora stared at him in disbelief. She had always looked up to Michael, never thought of him as stupid. Then again, where Maggie was concerned . . . "Can you possibly be so blind?"

Michael's face went through a range of emotions in a matter of moments. Starting with confusion, then disbelief, then sheer shock. He staggered back into the stall door as the impact of Nora's words struck him. "Are you saying that Maggie . . . That . . . James?"

Nora nodded. He really hadn't known. How could Maggie have kept this from him?

"And I'm the father?"

"No one else, Michael," Nora said softly.

"Did she tell you so herself?"

"She didn't have to."

Michael's hands flew to his head. "What an idiot I've been! How could she do this?"

"I thought she must have told you. I thought you'd come to this decision together—for Lady Darlington to claim James as her own. It can't have been easy for her," Nora pointed out. "She could have given the baby up while she was in France, but she didn't. At least she brought him home to be raised as a Darlington."

Still clutching his head, his expression stunned, Michael sank to the stable floor. "What am I to do, Nora? What should I do about this?"

"I don't see what you can do," Nora answered. "The best thing in my opinion is to do nothing."

"If I do nothing, how can I live with myself?"

"You're going to have to find a way," Nora insisted, "even if it's the hardest thing you ever do."

Abby Grahame

Chapter Seventeen

"YOU'RE A VERY GOOD RIDER," IAN PRAISED Lila as he cantered alongside her.

"Maggie's the horsewoman of the family," Lila said modestly though she was thrilled that he'd noticed her ability with a horse. She was used to being thoroughly in Maggie's shadow in equitation, as in most things, but since Ian had arrived, he'd paid attention only to Lila and she was glad that, at least, she'd worn Maggie's cast-off riding outfit with the cute high hat and the short nipped waist jacket. Although it was a hand-me-down, Ian had never seen it before, and Lila felt it showed her figure to good effect.

She had never felt more grown-up.

They were at the far end of the estate and Edmund

Marlborough's massive home was in view. Drawing to a halt, Ian emitted a long, low whistle of awed admiration. "What a place!" he remarked, gazing at the immense building.

"It's something, all right," Lila agreed, slowing beside him.

"Is your sister seriously thinking about marrying that guy?" Ian asked.

"I'm not sure. We're not as close as we were when we were younger. She no longer confides her thoughts on things like that to me. I can't believe she would be happy marrying someone so old, but it's possible she would sacrifice herself for the good of the family."

"And to go live in a place like that," Ian suggested. "Can you imagine? That place is grander than the White House."

"The where?" Lila asked.

"The capitol building in Washington," Ian explained.

"I should have realized," Lila said with an embarrassed laugh. It thrilled her that Ian never talked down to her and treated her as an equal. Since his return home, Wesley had been busy taking an informal inventory of Wentworth

Hall and its surroundings, no doubt to make suggestions to their father about what should be sold and what kept. This left Ian with a lot of time to spend with Lila, and she was loving every second of his attention. "I'd very much like to visit America some day. Wes told me he had a great visit with you."

"Perhaps you'll visit next," Ian suggested.

His words sent a thrill through her. Did he mean it? He seemed sincere. "That sounds wonderful," she replied.

"You'll love Newport," Ian went on. "The Astors have their summer place right near ours."

"That's so tragic about Mr. Astor dying on the *Titanic*," Lila commented, glad to have something knowledgeable to contribute.

"It is. I used to see him during yachting season. It's somehow fitting that he died at sea, since he was quite the sailor."

"I would love to learn to sail someday," Lila said, although the notion had only just come upon her at the moment.

Delight danced its way up her spine as Ian smiled at her. "I think it would be great fun to teach you how," he said, and she returned his smile. Apparently she had said exactly the right thing.

"Then you promise to teach me when I come to visit," Lila dared to press her luck.

"It's a promise," Ian replied.

As Lila and Ian sat on their horses, smiling at each other, Lila felt happier than she could remember feeling in a long time.

Maggie tried to block out the sound of the baby crying. But no matter how far down the hall she retreated, she couldn't block it. Where was Therese?

Why didn't someone go to James?

Unable to stand it another second, Maggie wheeled around and headed for the nursery. She found the baby kicking as he wailed in his crib. "There, there," she soothed as she bent to him. "I'm here." Instantly he calmed, turning toward her breast, even though the milk had dried in it months ago. Unexpected tears leaped to her eyes, one spilling down her cheek. He looked so much like Michael. It hurt to look at James just as it hurt to look at his father. It was exactly why she'd vowed to have nothing to do with him. It seemed like the right thing to do, but it was just so difficult.

"You're so beautiful, you look just like your daddy, don't you, sweetheart?" she whispered to the baby, rocking him in her arms.

Maggie brushed her wet eyes as her mother appeared in the doorway. "Why are you in here?" she asked.

"He's been left here to cry!" Maggie explained her presence. "Where is Therese?"

"Running down to the kitchen to get his infant formula, most likely." Lady Darlington shut the door behind her. "Maggie, we need to talk."

Lady Darlington spoke in an agitated whisper. "Quite clearly whomever wrote that last newspaper satire is implying that there has been some involvement between you and a gentleman. You've never told me who the father is, and I've taken your word that he is not someone who will make claims on James, who is now clearly a Darlington. But you must tell me who else might know about your . . . indescretion!"

Maggie knew she owed her mother a great deal. She'd helped Maggie through her secret pregnancy, had agreed to raise James as her own. Her mother had even lied to Lord Darlington about it. Not that her mother's motives had been entirely unselfish. If it came out that Maggie had had a child out of wedlock, the family name would be forever tarnished. All hope of her making a lucrative marriage would be dashed forever.

"Maggie, I feel forced to press you now that you've turned away both Teddy and the Duke. I must know who James's father is," Lady Darlington spoke in a whisper.

"It's as you assumed," Maggie lied, unable to meet her mother's gaze. "It was . . . someone I met during my come-out in London."

"Are you sure he doesn't know?"

"He has no idea."

"Is he a person you might consider marrying? Or . . . is he already married?"

"No! Absolutely not! But things are better as they are," Maggie replied. "Besides, I don't love him and he knows it."

Lady Darlington shook her head woefully. "If you don't love him, how did you let this happen?"

Maggie's mind raced. She needed a quick story and her

mother had taken her off guard with this line of questioning. "It was the champagne," she blurted out. "It made me feel giddy and romantic. It was my coming-out ball and I was eager for adult life to begin."

"Foolish girl," Lady Darlington lamented.

The wetness returned to Maggie's eyes. If her mother only knew how truly foolish she had been. She'd always loved Michael and their acting on that love had had an air of inevitability about it; all their lives had led to that one blissful encounter in the stable's hayloft. But then—on the very night she was about to tell him she was pregnant— Michael had broken it off, saying that the inequity in their stations made their romance impossible. He was always doing that—running hot and cold with her. He would tell her he was trying to protect her from a life of service, which would be inevitable if they were together. But a few kisses and he would warm right up again. That last night, she'd already learned of her pregnancy. So his coldness was more than she could bear. How could he claim he didn't love her? And then avoid her for weeks? That set her on a path leading to where they were today.

Why hadn't he taken her in his arms and said they

should run away together? She would have gone—in a heartbeat! Why did people have to be divided by something as arbitrary and heartless as their station in life? Now she couldn't leave. Not when James was at Wentworth Hall. She couldn't be a mother to him, but she would not abandon him.

What a right mess they had created!

Now Michael said he loved her and that he'd been wrong. Would he love her if he knew the truth? Maybe not. Even if they could never be together, the knowledge that she had his heart was a comfort. She would never do anything to jeopardize that. He could never know about James. Not ever.

No one could know.

If it came out that James was her baby, everything would be ruined: The Darlington name would tarnished forever; her chances of making a favorable match—one that the family desperately needed her to make—would be hopelessly dashed.

The consequence most distressing to Maggie would affect Lila. Before she even had her coming-out ball, her hopes of attracting a desirable beau would most certainly be destroyed. Her guilt was so immense it made being around Lila almost unbearably painful. She remembered how close they had been as girls and how much Lila had worshipped her. She had once basked in her younger sister's adoration, but since she'd returned home it only made her feel hypocritical, knowing she was unworthy of that worship. Maggie could never make herself forget that Lila's future might be utterly destroyed at any moment and it would be all her fault.

Maggie knew her aloof behavior hurt Lila to the core, but ultimately it was for Lila's own good. If she knew how Maggie had put Lila's whole life at risk, she would feel completely betrayed. It was better that there be some distance between them now. If the crack-up of their relationship came, the hurt wouldn't cut as deeply if there was already some distance between them.

The main problem, though, was that she missed Lila's companionship. It killed her that Lila thought Maggie was pushing her away and Maggie longed to explain what had happened. It could never be. For everyone's sake, Maggie had to keep the truth a secret, no matter what the cost.

"Maggie," Lady Darlington's voice cut through Maggie's thoughts. "You must tell me who this baby's father is. I thought we could let it go, but these newspaper pieces have changed all that. People will quickly figure out that they are skewering our family. Even if this paper is mostly read by the servant class, we all know servants gossip! We will be a laughingstock and our name forever ruined if this issue isn't quickly resolved. Tell me who it is, I beg of you. We can force this young man to marry you."

Maggie held James more tightly as she fought back another onslaught of tears. "I don't want him to marry me," she insisted in a choked voice, not meeting her mother's gaze, when all the while marrying this baby's father would have been her dearest wish come true.

Chapter Eighteen

THE KITCHEN WAS QUIET. DINNER HAD BEEN
served and cleaned up after. Most of the servants,
guests, and residents had returned to their quarters.
Nora and Michael were still up, finishing their suppers.
Nora rather enjoyed these moments—when the most you
could hear was the occasional cricket that had sneaked in
and one needn't worry about having to appear busy. During this time at night, the servants, with no one to wait
upon and nothing to clean, could be themselves. If they
weren't too exhausted.

"Blast these sewing needles," Nora muttered as she
picked at the calluses that had formed on her fingertips.

"How's the side job going?" asked Michael, peering
over his dinner at her fingertips.

Nora sighed, "Could be better if I wasn't so busy tending to all the goings-on around this bloody drafty place."

She poked her dinner with her fork, moving the potatoes and beef around the plate. Despite the insult that the servants were only permitted to eat meat left over from the meals prepared for the Darlingtons, the food was always prepared well and there was lots of it. Another plus was that, once dinner was over, no one really went into the kitchen, so it was a place to talk freely. Picking up a pea, she flicked it carelessly over Michael's shoulder. He ducked to avoid being hit with the green projectile.

In a swift motion, she watched Michael scoop up a handful of carrots. Nora quickly snatched up a napkin to shield herself from Michael's retaliatory fire. She continued talking from behind the white piece of cloth, "I can't even work back in my room because I can't have anyone seeing I have another job. It's ridiculous!"

"So what if they see? As long as you're getting your main duties done around here, who cares if you do a little extra sewing on the side?" Michael queried, tossing a piece of a carrot over Nora's napkin line of defense.

She let out a squeak of surprise as the carrot bounced

off her head and onto the floor. Lowering her cloth shield so just her eyes peered over, Nora replied, "I just don't want to chance it. I haven't saved up enough money to get to London yet and it'd be terrible if I got fired before that. I've only been taking jobs that I can finish on my one afternoon off and I give them back that day. Been working these fingers to the bone!" she said, letting the napkin fall, raising her hands and wiggling her rough fingertips to illustrate.

Michael nodded in sympathy, raising his own hands to show Nora the calluses on his palms from mucking stalls at the barn. "You're telling me!" He lowered his hands and scooped another helping of potatoes from the silver bowl onto his plate. "So, did you patch things up with Therese?"

Nora gave a half shrug, half nod, "I suppose. She said she was just nervous and didn't know what to say." She skeptically pouted her lips and continued on, "I mean, I *guess* I understand how she feels. She *is* the newest member of the staff and an outsider, after all."

Michael nodded, chewing thoughtfully. "She was probably just scared they would try and pin it on her," he mumbled through a mouthful of potatoes.

"Right," Nora agreed. "And, ignoring that one hang-up, Therese has been nothing but pleasant to me. I suppose I forgive her. Plus, that girl has a nose for gossip, so she could be a good ally."

Michael grinned. "Should you really trust a gossipy girl?"

Waving her hand dismissively, Nora said, "No! Of course n—" She stopped mid-sentence and glowered at Michael. "Very funny."

Laughing, Michael said, "I sure thought so."

Nora scowled, turning her head away in mock disgust. "At least I don't have spinach stuck in my teeth."

Michael's grin faded as he began to pick at his front teeth.

Nora clasped her hands together in front of her and leaned forward, happy to have the upper hand. "So. Now about you. You know the baby is yours. What're you going to do?"

Michael took a deep breath, clasped his hands behind his head, and rocked on the back two legs of his chair. Sighing, he said, "I . . . don't know." Staring at the ceiling, he continued on: "On the one hand, the baby is clearly better off being a Darlington. Even in their reduced circumstances, they could provide so much for him. I don't think I'd be able to give him the same opportunities in life. But, on the other hand, I absolutely cannot stand to see *my* son being raised falsely by another person." He looked down from the ceiling, catching Nora's eyes. "I want to talk to Maggie about it, but she has been avoiding me like the plague."

Nora nodded, contemplatively tapping her fork against her lips. Slowly, she said, "Do you want me to send a message to her?"

Letting the front two legs of his chair regain contact with the floor with a loud clack, Michael looked at Nora. "Would you do that for me?"

"Of course!" she replied naturally, and then thinking better of it, feigned disinterest. "Well, then again, word on the *street*," she said pointedly, staring into Michael's eyes to drive home her point, "is that gossipy girls aren't to be trusted, even though they have all of the ins and could easily deliver important information. . . ." She gazed off somewhere in the distance, trying to suppress a grin.

"Do it for me," Michael said in a gentle command, half-teasing and half-serious.

"And what if I refuse?" replied Nora, rubbing at her face with the napkin, "I'm not so keen on doing favors for food-flinging ruffians such as yourself."

"Well," Michael started, leaning forward, "what if I was to tell you *and* the entire staff *and* the Darlingtons that I knew a bit of insider information."

Nora narrowed her eyes at him. "You wouldn't dare."

"Oh, wouldn't I?" Michael grinned back at her. As much as Nora viewed him as a brother, Michael viewed her as a sister. Specifically, a little sister whom he loved to ruffle up as she did to him, although deep down they knew their intentions were nothing but kind for one another. "Oh, yes. From what I hear there is a young maid who has been doing some extra sewing work on the side and not telling her Lordship about the money she has been saving to go to . . . where was it? Oh, yes, London . . ."

Jumping up from her seat, Nora raced around the table, shoving her napkin over Michael's mouth. Even though all of the staff were in their rooms, she couldn't help but feel a stab of panic. "Ssh! Stop it!" she hissed. "I'll do it, I'll do it!" She could hear Michael's muffled chuckles coming from beneath the fabric. He reached up and gently removed her clamped hand from over his mouth, letting the napkin fall into his lap.

She plopped down in the seat next to him and stuck out her bottom lip, trying to muster up false indignation. "I was going to do it anyway. You know I care about you and Maggie."

Michael shifted in his seat to face her and patted her hand, still chuckling. He focused his intense eyes upon her. "And I thank you for it. This means so much to me, thank you."

Nora looked deeply into his eyes, as if studying his level of sincerity. She took a deep breath and let it out slowly, patting his hand back. "You know you are a supreme git, don't you?" Her face broke into a grin.

"Oh, just write the sodding letter for me, would you?" He retorted, snatching up the napkin and tossing it at her.

"All right, all right, down to business," she replied, laughing. Striding across the kitchen to where the cookbooks were kept, she ripped a blank page out of a notebook and grabbed a pen. Returning, she pounded the piece of paper down upon the table for dramatic effect and stared pointedly at Michael. "Spill your heart out and I'll deliver this letter to your fair maiden, words transcribed 'pon this parchment, tucked safely inside a book, and delivered for only your miss to see."

"You really have a sense for theatrics, don't you?"

Nora adjusted the pen in her hand, ready to write. "All the world's a stage, as they say. Now spill it."

Chapter Nineteen

WESLEY FOUND HIMSELF RUNNING down the long drive leading into Wentworth Hall. He hadn't meant to break into a run, but it was as though his legs had a will of their own. The object of his chase was Therese, who was only a few yards ahead of him. He'd spied her leaving the estate and gone out after her, filled with an overwhelming desire to accompany the young woman whom he found exquisite in every way, from her delicate beauty to the melodious, French-accented voice that flowed from her bowed lips. He had to be near her.

She had seemed so curious about him when they had first set eyes on each other. But he couldn't mistake her coldness when he visited her in the nursery. She must have assumed he was toying with her, that he was a typical high-born Lord looking to tumble a member of his staff. He would have to convince her otherwise. His time in America had led him to have a much more progressive view of the social classes. What did a title really mean, anyway?

"*Bonjour*, Monsieur Wesley," Therese greeted him as he strode breathlessly to her side.

"Good day to you, Therese," Wesley answered brightly. "Where are you off to on this dreary day?" he asked, pointing up to the thunderclouds rolling ominously overhead.

"I have the morning off, and so I am walking into town to post some letters to friends in Paris."

"There is no love letter there to some fortunate young man, I hope," Wesley said as he walked alongside. Though he kept his tone buoyant and teasing his question was not really a joke. If Therese had a love back in France he wanted to know. If so, he intended to make her forget all about it.

"No, monsieur. There is no such fellow," Therese answered.

"Would you like there to be?" Wesley probed.

Therese glanced at him questioningly from the corners of her eyes.

"I ask only because I need to know if I have a chance with you," Wesley admitted boldly. "Would you mind if I accompany you into town?"

"There is no need for that," Therese replied. "It is not far."

"Wouldn't you like company, just the same?"

Therese let out a quick sigh. "It is not necessary."

Her reluctance puzzled Wesley. He didn't consider himself a snob, but what servant would not welcome the attentions of the lord of the manor? Through the years he'd flirted with some of the maids and never before been rebuffed. And even among his own class, girls usually found his company pleasant. He wasn't interested in any of those young women, though. Therese was the one he found himself thinking about day and night.

"Don't you like me, Therese?" Wesley asked. "I hope you do, because I like you. I like you very much."

"It is not fitting for us to be friends," Therese responded tersely, keeping her sights glued to the path ahead of them.

"This is the modern world, Therese," Wesley countered. "I've just spent the summer in America with Ian and perhaps

I've picked up some more contemporary idea from our friends in the New World. In America no one has titles and it simply doesn't matter. It's what you make of yourself that counts over there, not some archaic title one was born with."

"Well, we are in Europe, and here it matters," Therese pointed out, still unable to meet his eyes.

"I see!" Wesley exclaimed. She really did believe he was toying with her, trying to secretly seduce a pretty young member of the staff for his own lecherous purposes. "I'm not like that, Therese," he said persuasively. "My intentions are sincere. And I don't care who knows it."

Therese let out a light snort of disbelief.

"You don't believe me?" he asked warmly.

She shrugged.

"Then allow me to prove it." They were nearly to the front gate and no one from the estate would be able to see them. Wesley stopped her short and stared into her eyes. She shifted uncomfortably. When his face slowly began descending toward hers she stepped back abruptly.

"Stop!" Therese cried, banging on his chest with a quick, hard blow that sent him reeling back several steps. "Stop this moment!"

"Do you find me that repulsive, Therese?" Wesley asked, more hurt than angry.

"There can never be anything between us," Therese insisted in a heated tone. "Never! Never!"

"You're the snob, not me," Wesley shot back. "I am not thinking about your station in life. I see only you, a beautiful young woman who haunts my every waking hour. But you don't see me. You see only my title, and you hold against me something I have no control over."

"It is not your title that makes it impossible," Therese told him passionately. "It is not what is different about us that must divide us. It is what we share."

"What might that be?" Wesley demanded.

"A father!" Therese replied, her voice rising to a near shout.

"What?"

Therese simply glared at him, as if waiting for him to catch up.

Wesley had heard her words but his mind had trouble making sense of them. "My father?"

Dumbstruck and slack-jawed with amazement, Wesley listened as Therese unfurled a story he would never have believed if he wasn't hearing it from her own lips. Nineteen years earlier her mother had worked in Wesley's aunt's household. "There she met your father who seduced her. When she confronted him about her fears she was pregnant, he wanted nothing to do with her. You see, he had a wife and newborn son of his own. She went to Lady Daphne and admitted she was in trouble, but never said who the father was. She let her believe it was a commoner. Lady Daphne took pity on her and let her stay in her household, even taking her to France when she moved."

Wesley's mind reeled. He could hardly believe his father would do such a thing: the old hypocrite, always so proper and stiff. He never would have believed his father capable of such callous behavior.

He studied Therese closely and suddenly saw a family resemblance he had never noticed until this moment. The shape of her face was exactly the same as Maggie's. Her arched brows were like Lila's. And, with a shudder he realized that the blue of her eyes mirrored his own. How could he have missed these things before? Now in the grip of this new vision, there could be no question that her story was true.

Therese continued her tale. "No one but you knows that I am Lord Darlington's daughter, except Lord Darlington himself."

"My father knows you're his child and yet he has kept you as a servant?" he questioned incredulously.

"I confronted Lord Darlington a few weeks after I arrived, telling him who I am. He didn't deny it. But he refused to acknowledge me, even after knowing that my mother had died and I had no one left."

"He wouldn't give you the Darlington name, even after learning who you are?"

"No, he simply told me that if I mentioned to anyone who I am, he would send me home to Paris at once."

A roll of thunder made both Therese and Wesley check the dark clouds overhead. "You'd better turn back," Wesley suggested. "It's about to storm." As if on cue, wind whipped up around them, ruffling Therese's skirts and Wesley's jacket.

As light rain moistened her face, Therese and Wesley looked at each other, each studying the other. There were indeed storms coming, Wesley thought.

* * *

"Lady Lila," Nora started. "Has there been any new information about the satires?"

"What?" Lila answered, distracted. She was seated on her settee lazily brushing her hair, while Nora set out her clothes for supper. Her head had been in the clouds lately, probably the fault of a certain young American. "Oh, those things. I haven't heard a thing about them lately. Why do you ask?"

"Well, it's just that I've been searching my mind about them. I need you to know I have been racking my brain to find out who could have betrayed your family in this way. And I can't help but think it has to be Miss Jessica," she suggested.

"Why?" Lila asked, wide-eyed with surprised disbelief.

"She's always scribbling in that notebook and she's so secretive about what's inside. It seems to me that she's taking notes for her satires. Doesn't that make sense?"

"Not entirely," Lila disagreed. "What would she stand to gain by mocking us like that?"

"She's simply mean-spirited," Nora countered. "Her type doesn't need a reason to be cruel. It's in her nature."

"I think that's harsh, Nora," Lila insisted.

Abby Grahame

"Maybe it is. Just the same, she gets my vote as the most likely culprit."

"It does feel odd not knowing who was behind them. Especially since it's clear they were written by someone under our roof! It's chilling to think someone we know and trust could do such a thing." Folding her arms pensively, Lila pouted. "If only we could get a peek into that notebook."

Maggie appeared in the open doorway. "What notebook?"

"Nora thinks Jessica is taking notes about our family in that notebook she always carries," Lila explained.

"You think she's our evil satirist?" Maggie inquired, stepping into the room and perching on the end of Lila's bed.

"That's my opinion," Nora confirmed.

"How can we catch her at it?" Maggie wondered.

Lila looked at Maggie, her brows arched in thought, her chin propped on her hands. It reminded her of the old days when they were united in trying to figure a way out of some dilemma: how to sneak out to play in the stable with Michael and Nora, or the best way to sneak extra pie from the kitchen. These memories warmed her, and she felt a sudden outpouring of love for her older sister as well as a deep desire to be united in some new scheme with her. "How can we get our hands on that notebook?" she questioned.

"I just left Jessica reading in the library, reading a novel," Maggie replied. "Why don't you go down there and engage her in conversation. Make sure she doesn't leave the room. That will give me time to snoop around her bedroom for the notebook. She didn't have it with her in the library."

Lila grinned, intrigued by the idea. It was so good to be embroiled in one of Maggie's schemes once more.

"All right. I'll get going to Jessica's room," Maggie suggested to Lila. "You head off to the library."

"What should I do?" Nora asked.

"Come with me and be the lookout in case Teddy comes by or Jessica escapes Lila."

"Will do," Nora agreed.

"We're off," Maggie said as she headed for the door. "Good luck."

"I'll be fine," Lila assured her.

As soon as Maggie and Nora departed, Lila noticed a

Abby Grahame

novel sitting on the dresser: *Oliver Twist* by Charles Dickens. Nora must have meant to bring it back up to the library but forgotten it. As long as she was heading for the library herself she might as well bring it up. Tucking the volume under her arm, she set out for her encounter with Jessica.

Maggie stood in Jessica's room, wondering where to start looking. Crossing to the vanity, she pulled open all the drawers but discovered nothing. Pushing up the sides of the pink silk covers, she ran her hands between the mattress and the box spring along the entire bed, but with no success. Then, struck with a sudden inspiration, she tossed the pillows from the head to the center of the bed. "Voilà!" she murmured, seizing upon the red journal.

Stepping out into the hall, she held up the red journal to show Nora—who had busied herself dusting the tall, gilt picture frames—that she'd uncovered her prize. Nora smiled and nodded.

Back inside the room, Maggie fanned through the pages until, halfway through, the neat, tight handwriting stopped. She started by reading the last entry first:

Just weeks now until Teddy and I turn eighteen. Thank

God! *The first thing I intend to do when my inheritance comes through is to return to Johannesburg. I am so homesick and have had it with living here with the Darlingtons. Lila and Maggie remind me of all those titled brats. They are just the same sorts of snobs who plagued me while I was in London during my debutante season. They were just as concerned about their "names" and family lineage, mocking Teddy and me just because we aren't descended from some musty old family covered in cobwebs. I'm proud that our father made his fortune on his own rather than inheriting it.*

My mother, too, came from Dutch South Africans who farmed to make their fortune. How I wish I had known her better. I'm certain she would have loathed the stuffiness of English society. In that way I am truly her daughter.

After reading several earlier pages, Maggie sighed, shutting the notebook and laying the pillows back over it. They were certainly uninformative and disappointing, though they did explain Jessica's haughty disdain. The bad reception she'd been given in London had set her against the English aristocracy, which the Darlingtons represented to her.

Nora had convinced her that Jessica was the author

of the satires, but there wasn't a word in the journal about Jessica having written them. And more importantly, no observations about the Darlingtons that indicated she'd uncovered any of their secrets. The only mention of the satires was one entry where Jessica confessed that she found the pieces hilarious and accurate, implying that the Darlingtons deserved the mockery they were getting. When Maggie read that, anger put red blotches into her cheeks, but it didn't prove that Jessica had authored the newspaper pieces.

If it wasn't Jessica, then who was it?

Lila wasn't even close to the library when she heard Jessica's laughter tinkling like chimes down the hallway. She realized that in the whole time Jessica had been at Wentworth Hall, Lila had never heard Jessica as much as giggle, not even once. What could be the cause of this merriment?

Upon entering the library, Lila came upon Jessica smiling flirtatiously at Ian, who sat on the other end of the leather couch regaling her with a tale of some sailing mishap. Lila was struck with a hard snap of jealousy. Why was Jessica standing so close to Ian? It certainly appeared that Jessica was enjoying his company—she was friendlier to him than she'd ever been to any of the Darlingtons.

"Lila!" Ian greeted her with a smile.

The lively shine in Jessica's eyes dulled into annoyance. "Hello, Lila," she said stiffly.

"What have you got there?" Ian inquired with a nod at the book tucked in Lila's hand.

"Oliver Twist," Lila reported.

"That's one of my favorite books," Ian revealed with enthusiasm. "How are you liking it?"

"I love it!" Lila fibbed, wanting to strike a common bond with him. "I came up here to read it. I had no idea anyone was in here."

"Don't let us stop you from reading," Jessica said without warmth. Clearly her intent was to keep Lila from joining their conversation.

"Yes, don't let us keep you from it," Ian agreed. "When I was reading *Oliver Twist*, I was aggravated by any interruption to my progress. All I wanted to do was get on with the story. Do sit and read. I'll keep my voice down. Can you concentrate if we keep talking?"

"Of course," Lila said, settling into the hunter green leather high-backed chair across from the couch. She suddenly wanted to devour the novel as quickly as possible so that she would have some reason to talk to him. Besides that, her goal was to keep Jessica occupied and Ian was doing a better job of it than she ever could. "Continue telling Jessica your story and I'll settle in here to read," she said. "You won't bother me."

"Yes, do tell me the rest," Jessica said brightly. "I'm dying to hear how this ends."

Lila opened the book and immediately came upon a piece of lined paper folded in thirds. Curious, she undid it and saw it was a letter addressed to Maggie. Turning it revealed that it was from Michael. With darting eyes, she raced through it:

My Most Dear Maggie,

I write you today begging your forgiveness. I have been an insensitive fool and caused you great pain. I don't know how I could have been so blind to have not realized that I am the father of darling little James. It angered me at first to think you had kept this from me. But now that my eyes have been opened, it fills me with remorse that you have had to go though so much on your own without my help or support. You are such a brave and strong person. You could have easily given our boy up for adoption but you chose instead to make sure he would be raised under your watchful eye as a member of your own family. This touches me deeply and fills me with the greatest respect for you.

One thing I do not regret is the night of love we shared that produced our son. Had I known he was conceived, I would have moved Heaven and Earth to make a life for us. Now that I do know, I humbly ask you for that chance. You would be giving up so much, but I would treat you like a queen in a way that no duke or earl could match. If you will accept me as your husband, I swear I will spend the rest of my days endeavoring to make you and little James the two happiest people on the planet. It's true we have many obstacles, but I know we can set everything to right as long as we are together.

Love,

Michael

By the time she was reading the last lines, tears were welling in Lila's eyes. Poor Maggie! Poor Michael! She felt ashamed that she had been so angry with her sister. Of course she hadn't wanted Lila along on the trip to France. It made perfect sense now. She had gone abroad to conceal her pregnancy. What a lonely, frightening time she must have had. Their mother had been with her, but she was not exactly a warm, comforting presence. In fact, their mother's disapproving coldness must have been more of a torment than a help to Maggie. No wonder her elder sister had become just a shell of herself.

What would become of them? They surely deserved more happiness than they were getting. How was it fair that they be denied happiness? Just because Michael didn't have a title? Fat lot of good having a title was doing the Darlingtons these days!

"What's going on, Lila?" Ian asked, looking at her with a puzzled, concerned expression. "You look so distressed. Are you to the part where Nancy gets murdered?"

He'd jolted Lila from her reverie and she looked up at him sharply. It took her a moment to understand what he'd said. "Oh, no, n-not yet," she stammered. Seeing him reminded her of what he'd said the other day: that in America people were free to make their own fortunes. If Maggie went to America with Michael and the baby, could they also rise on their own merits? It seemed to her that they deserved the chance to at least try.

Chapter Twenty ✦

DESPITE ALL OF HIS YEARS WORKING AS a groom, Michael still took a certain solace in being around horses. He paused as he walked toward the stables to watch the horses grazing in the green pasture. Heads down, nibbling at the grass, they looked so calm and content. Michael sighed—oh, to be a horse. To not have to deal with the issues of being a human. To not have to worry about money, and society, and love . . . Michael sighed once again, shaking his head as if to shoo away his daydream, and continued walking toward the barn.

The familiar pungent smell of hay and horse sweat greeted his nostrils as he approached the stalls. He considered it a good thing that there was always so much work to be done around the barn. It kept his mind off troubling matters around the manor. He opened the creaky door to the tack room, where he was suddenly greeted by an unexpected sight.

"Lila! What are you doing here?"

Lila didn't move from her sitting spot on top of an old tack box. She raised her head slowly to meet Michael's eyes. "I have a plan," she said in a more serious tone than Michael had ever heard her use before.

"A plan?" he asked as he entered the small, dusty room. He now wondered how much Lila knew, and how much she had pieced together after overhearing him and Maggie the night of the duke's ball. Suddenly self-conscious, he strode forth and picked up a saddle off one of the racks, bracing it against his hip as he searched the line of bridles hung up on the wall to find the corresponding one.

Lila jumped up from her seat, shedding her air of contemplation and donning one of action. Snatching an equally grimy brown leather bridle off of the wall, she held it out for Michael. He paused before taking it, hand outstretched, yet hesitant to take it from her, as if there would be some unforeseen catch if he were to do so.

"What, may I ask, is this epic plan regarding?" he asked slowly, hand still wavering in the air.

Lila plopped the dusty bridle into his open hand. "You and Maggie. I have a way for you two to be together."

His expression changed from one of tentative interest to one of exasperation. Exhaling loudly and spinning on his heel toward the door, he took a step forward but was blocked by a quick-moving Lila. She stood in the door frame, arms braced against the wood, making it clear she wouldn't let him through until he heard her out.

"You shouldn't be involved in this, Lila," he said.

"Don't be ridiculous. She's my sister. And she loves you. The real kind of love that doesn't go away when it's no longer fun. Besides, my plan is quite good!" Lila insisted, shifting slightly to the left as Michael tried to duck under her arm. Blocking him, she added, "You knew the old version of my sister. She was adventurous, wild, and reckless. Someone like that doesn't just change."

Michael stepped back, his eyes squaring up Lila. "Whatever this plan is of yours, how do you know Maggie will go for it?"

"Haven't you been listening? Because she loves you," Lila said simply, allowing her arms to drop from the door frame. Michael brushed past her and into the barn aisle. Lila scurried after him. "I know my sister. What's more, I know I can *convince* my sister to go along with this plan. But *you* have to be willing to do it."

Michael tossed the saddle and bridle down upon the aisle floor, a small cloud of dust rising in the air as he did. "And what, pray tell, is this ingenious plan of yours?" He was growing frustrated with being reminded of the unfortunate situation he was in. It had taken so much for him to finally give up hope. The notion that he and Maggie could someday be together just brought up feelings of bitter pain now. And here Lila was, bothering him about it.

"You're just going to have to trust me." Lila insisted, sincerity in her voice.

"Why? Why should I just trust you?" Michael asked, spitting the word "trust" out like it tasted bad. "I've been through enough. Don't go getting my hopes up for a plan that will just fall apart."

"Because this is your final chance to do something to save you and Maggie. The only thing you have to do is trust me," Lila pleaded, reaching forward and grasping his hand to drive home her point. "Just trust me," she whispered, staring pleadingly into his eyes.

Michael stared back, arms crossed. He opened his mouth to reply, but was cut off by a cough with a decided point to it, clear someone was making his or her entrance known. Whirling around, the pair's eyes landed upon Wesley.

"Sorry. Was I . . . interrupting something?" Wesley asked, eyes drifting from Lila to Michael and back again. Michael let out a loud, short laugh, removing his hand from Lila's grasp.

"Not at all. Lila was just leaving, weren't you, Lila?" Michael asked, tilting his head at her.

Lila gave one last imploring look at Michael, hoping to make her point clear without words. "Yes. I was just leaving, indeed. Michael," she said, addressing him head-on, "I will be seeing you later."

Giving no reply, Michael directed his attention to Wesley as Lila strode stiffly out of the barn. Wesley toyed with a piece of broken wood that was hanging from one of the stall doors. With his shoulders slumped forward and a distant look in his eyes, Michael wondered what was wrong with him.

"M'lord?" asked Michael softly as he stepped closer to the distracted-looking man.

Wesley jumped at the sound of Michael's voice. Startled, he said, "Oh! Yes. Uhm . . . please get my horse ready for me. I think I should like to go for a ride. A distraction would be marvelous about now. "

Michael nodded. "Right away, m'lord."

Therese's shoes clacked softly against the cold tile floor. Her breath was shallow as her nerves drew tense for the conversation that was about to occur. Now that Wesley knew the truth, she couldn't stay here. Once Wesley confronted his . . . *their* father, she would be out on the streets. Which meant Therese had to talk to Lord Darlington before Wesley did. It was the only way.

She drew in a deep, steadying breath as she raised her fist to knock upon Lord Darlington's study door. Exhaling, she gave three short raps upon the dark mahogany. Therese winced slightly as the noise reverberated throughout the large hallway. There was a long pause and no one answered.

Lord Darlington is always in his study at this time . . . , she mused. Biting her lower lip, she raised a tentative fist to the door again, drew back her wrist, and prepared for another knock.

A muffled, but angry-sounding, voice came from within. "Yes, come in, who is it?"

Jumping slightly at the sound of his voice, Therese opened the door with a gulp.

"Lord Darlington?" asked Therese timidly, trying to muster bravado as she entered his study.

"Clearly, it is. Who else would it be?" Lord Darlington responded flatly, cold eyes boring into hers.

Therese, taken aback by his rudeness, fumbled to find the right words. Her eyes darted about the dusty study. Bookshelves lined the walls and there was a crackling fire to his right. Shadows were cast against the walls and they danced and played with the fire's motion. The windows were covered with dark, crimson velvet drapes. Lord Darlington sat in a high-backed chair behind a desk that was covered in files and papers.

"Well, out with it, girl!" Lord Darlington snapped. "I haven't all day to stare at you staring at me."

Abby Grahame

Therese nodded her head firmly, choosing to be blunt. "I would like to leave Wentworth Hall," she said, trying to sound as decisive as possible.

"Well, then, thank you for your time and ask one of the maids to help you with your belongings on your way out," Lord Darlington replied, lowering his gaze back to the papers on his desk, gathering and hitting a stack back into organized submission with a firm thump.

"I will leave as soon as I receive enough money to set myself up in my own establishment in London," Therese said, gaining confidence.

Not raising his eyes from the desk, Lord Darlington arched a single eyebrow. "I'm sorry to inform you that cannot be arranged at this time." He lifted his eyes from his paper. "Good day and have a safe trip back to Paris."

"I'm not leaving until I receive my proper sum. If you do not comply, I will tell Lady Darlington the truth about my mother."

Lord Darlington slowly raised his eyes to meet with Therese's. His look was a combination of fury, belittling amusement, and confusion. Therese instinctively took a step backward.

"Is that so?" he asked, rising from his desk and standing up straight at full height. With his starched and pressed appearance and stern mannerisms, he was very intimidating.

Therese resisted the urge to shrink backward any farther. She was tempted to run from the room, but knew what had to be done was imperative to her livelihood. Knowing this would likely be the last time she ever saw him, Therese had to ask, "How could you turn your back on your own child?"

Lord Darlington had no response, but a look of shame crossed his features for the briefest moment.

"When I came to you to explain who I was, I did not ask for money. Or a title. I only wanted a father."

"How was I to know your mother was telling the truth?" Lord Darlington bellowed. "Many high-born men have been fooled."

"I am standing before you now. Do you not see a resemblance? Can you be so hard-hearted?"

"This from a girl who is trying to extort from me? No, you could never be a Darlington. Our behavior would never be so low."

Therese felt ice start to flow through her veins. She hated him. He was so in love with his status he couldn't see beyond it. Well, soon the Darlington name would be in complete disrepute. Even the Darlingtons wouldn't want the Darlington name.

Nodding, she said, "Sir, if you do not do as I ask, I will be forced to inform her of your rather unbecoming behavior."

Lord Darlington studied her for a moment, as if considering how to handle the situation. Finally a strange smile broke over his face. "Go ahead. Do it," he sniffed, appearing suddenly disinterested. "It's not uncommon for a lord to have illegitimate children. My lady would forgive me. After all, it was almost two decades ago. Old news."

Therese was taken aback. She didn't expect him to say such things . . . to be so certain. Straightening her back and squaring her shoulders, she shot back, "Fine. *She* may forgive you. But will society when I tell the newspapers an even better bit of information?" Eyes ablaze, she locked gazes with Lord Darlington, hoping to convey that she would not back down.

"And what information would that be?" he countered, folding his arms over his chest.

Therese paused, unsure if she should divulge this secret. Decisively, she shot back, "That baby James isn't your son . . . but your grandson. He belongs to none other than your daughter Maggie. Oh, yes," Therese continued on, seeing she now had the upper hand due to Lord Darlington's inability to mask his shock, "Your lady lied to you. She covered up for your daughter. Did you really think a woman of her age could bear a child? And didn't you notice Maggie's behavior after she came back from France? How she looked at that baby?"

Lord Darlington blinked a few times, studying Therese. "There is no way anyone would believe those lies."

"Lies? Lies! The only person who is lying here is *you* to *yourself*. I do not speak lies about this matter. Plus, the newspapers will gleefully print this information. They do not care if it is true or not. They obviously haven't cared what the truth was in the past. This will ruin you and you know it!" Therese stated, index finger jabbing the air in front of Lord Darlington's chest, her own chest heaving up and down after her passionate monologue.

With a quick intake of breath, he raised his hand into the air. Flushed red with anger, his hand froze, quivering in midair. Chin held high, she winced, but held her ground, waiting for the coming blow. The tension in the air was palpable as a few heartbeats passed between them. Lowering his hand, Lord Darlington scowled at Therese, knowing she was correct.

He returned to his seat at the desk, face still red with fury. Tensely, he opened a locked drawer in his desk and began removing a few items.

"You will receive a sum of two hundred pounds. Half I have, and the rest will be paid in jewels, which you can hawk as you please once you are far and away from Wentworth. You are to leave *now*. Not in a few hours, not tomorrow morning, but *now*. There is a ferry leaving Southampton in a few hours and you are to be present for it," he concluded, giving intent focus to the files upon his desk, refusing to look her in the eyes. "Gerald will personally escort you. Again, you are to have contact with no one and *leave immediately*. You will receive your money and jewels once my butler sees that you are properly on the ferry and never to come back or even breathe a word that you had worked here previously. Is that understood?"

Therese stifled a small squeak of triumph, holding a winning grin back with all of her might. She diverted her eyes toward her shoes, hoping to affect a demure and grateful appearance. "Yes, sir."

"Good. Now get out of my study!" he finished with a snap, finally looking up at her.

"Yes, sir. Right away . . ." She exited toward the door, slipping out of the dark frame into the hallway. Before she shut the door, she ducked her head back in and added, "I mean, yes, *father*." And with that, slammed the door behind her.

Chapter Twenty-One

LORD DARLINGTON FUMED TO HIMSELF AS he paced from wall to wall in his study. He had never thought his past mistakes would come back to haunt him in this most egregious manner. What if that little French girl was bluffing? She must have been. Also, his wife would never dare lie to him like that . . . and what's more, his daughter, though so often reckless, had matured and would have never have been so careless with both her own body *and* the family name!

He had to confront Lady Darlington. But he needed to wait to make sure Therese was gone first.

Once Gerald returned to the study and nodded that Therese had left, Lord Darlington stalked out, slamming the thick mahogany door on his way out. He walked quickly to the garden hothouse, where his wife was so often to be found.

Lady Darlington stood there, sunbonnet over her dark salt-and-pepper hair, trimming a small rosebush. She hummed softly to herself as she snipped at the pungent red flowers. She wore a flowing yellow dress that covered her, yet gracefully clung to her figure. Lord Darlington stopped at the entrance and studied his wife's body.

Although she had a mature frame, one that had produced three children, it was not the body of a woman who had just brought a newborn into the world. He had seen his wife post-child—her hips appearing wider, breasts plump with milk, and face fuller from nine months of providing food to her baby within. Besides a few extra wrinkles upon her face, Lady Darlington possessed none of these postpartum traits.

Pursing his lips, he spoke out, "Tell me the truth."

Surprised, Lady Darlington jumped, and in doing so, snipped a rose too short and caught her finger in the process. "Ouch!" she exclaimed, brows furrowing as she turned quickly to see who had spoken. Putting her damaged finger to her lip, blood seeping down the side, she mumbled back to her husband, "About what?"

"The baby," he replied flatly, looking stiffer than ever. His hands stuck to his hips and his face exuded irritation.

"What about James?" she asked, moving to find a bandage for her finger.

"Who is his mother?" Lord Darlington responded, not moving, flinching, or hesitating.

Lady Darlington stopped searching for the bandage, her back to her husband. Pausing, trying to think of the best words, she stammered out her answer, "What . . . whatever do you mean?"

Lord Darlington stepped forward. With wide, meaningful strides, he walked up in front of his wife. Fear entered her eyes as she watched him forcefully grab her wrists and hold them up beside her face. His body quivered with rage, his face turning a deep red. Lady Darlington's eyes widened, her husband's face not inches from hers. She glanced up to see a vein in his temple throbbing. She had not seen him this angry in years, and possibly ever.

"Don't play coy with me!" he snarled, enraged spit flying from his lips. "Who. Is. The. Baby's. Mother?" he said, punctuating each word, his voice reaching a crescendo of rage.

Trying to wriggle out of her husband's grip, Lady Darlington winced at the pain coming from her wrists. "Unhand me!" she cried, twisting her face away from him.

"No! Not until you tell me the truth!" he spat, his grip tightening over his wife's petite wrists.

Lady Darlington stared at him, pupils dilating out of fear. She took a quivering breath, trying to regain her composure. She looked her husband square in the eye. "You're *hurting* me."

He paused and gave her wrists one last meaningful squeeze before tossing her aside. "Well, you've hurt me. How could you lie? *Why* would you lie?" he asked, turning his back to her.

Lady Darlington massaged her wrists, brows knit together in pain, her finger still bleeding. Blood gently seeped down her hand and onto the floor. Realizing Lord Darlington had already come to the conclusion in his own mind, she fought back tears of fright, anger, and humiliation.

"To save the family name and Maggie's future. You know just as well as I do that if she had a child out of wedlock, the papers would run our name through the mud.

Abby Graham

She'd never be able to find a suitable husband, and maybe even little Lila would be adversely affected," she said, trying to keep her voice from shaking.

"Who is the father?" Lord Darlington asked, hands balling into fists.

"I don't know," she replied, her back still to him.

"Who is the father?" he asked once more, wheeling on his heel and facing his wife.

"I. Don't. Know," she responded, watching as Lord Darlington walked back over, quickly closing his proximity to her.

"Who is the father? Stop covering for her!" he shouted into her face, so close that she could smell his breath.

Palm out, she pulled back and with a quick smack, slapped Lord Darlington across the cheek. Eyes boring into each other, they waited for the other to make a move. Afraid, Lady Darlington wondered if she had made a dreadful mistake.

With a voice barely above a whisper, she said, "I told you. I don't know. Maggie refused to tell me who the father is."

A handprint was slowly beginning to form in red over

Lord Darlington's already crimson face. "And this is the truth?" he asked, his voice a husky whisper.

Lady Darlington nodded and recommenced massaging her bruised wrists. "I wish I knew who the father of my first grandchild was as well, but Maggie absolutely will not speak of him."

Lord Darlington nodded slowly. "I see. Well, I am sure I can find a way to make her speak the truth."

"She's liked a locked safe. You're not going to get anything from her. Believe me, I've tried," replied Lady Darlington.

Lord Darlington shifted and began to walk from the room, his voice thick with emotion. "You haven't tried like I will. Oh, she'll speak. She'll speak if it's the last thing she does. . . ."

Lila jogged across the expansive green lawn toward Wentworth Hall. This plan was going to work. It *had* to work. It was the last chance for Maggie, Michael, and baby James to be together, to be a happy family with a new start.

She stopped and considered what she was about to

do. It was such a bold move. And it would cost her. Her parents would probably be furious. They might never even forgive her. But Wes would be onboard. She could count on him, and even if they never forgave her, Lila knew Wes wouldn't turn his back on her. He'd make sure she'd never be left penniless.

It had to be done. It was the right thing to do.

It was the *only* thing to do.

Wiping the sweat from her brow, Lila took a deep breath as she pushed open one of the heavy doors leading into Wentworth Hall. The last piece of the puzzle to her plan lay inside. Before going to Maggie, she had to convince one last person of this plan. She had to find Ian, and she had to find him fast. Time was of the essence—if she didn't move quickly, all could be lost in a matter of moments. Hopefully, Ian and his motorcar would be willing to be of help.

Chapter Twenty-Two

SOMETHING SIGNIFICANT HAD HAPPENED. Every instinct for gossip that Nora possessed told her so. She'd seen Therese earlier rushing back to the servants quarters and the girl wouldn't meet anyone's eyes. Wesley was brooding on a long walk in the fields, and had opted not to take Ian. Lord Darlington's face was scrunched into a permanent scowl and someone had quite obviously slapped him across the face. Lila had come in and darted up the stairs, seemingly in a frantic search for something or someone. Lady Darlington was lost in thought and kept rubbing her wrists. Maggie was nowhere to be seen at all.

The result was that Nora found herself squirming in a torment of curiosity. She had to get the facts on this situation. That all this activity was swirling around her and that she hadn't a clue to what was going on was completely unacceptable.

She would speak to Therese. Nora sensed that somehow she was at the heart of this. She checked in the nursery and found the baby fast asleep. During those breaks, Therese often went to read or write letters in her bedroom. Climbing the stairs to the servants' quarters, Nora resolved to demand the truth from the girl.

She entered their room to find the drawers of every dresser had been pulled open and emptied, and the top of Therese's dresser had been cleared of everything that had been there except for several sheets of paper folded together. Therese must have left behind one of those letters home that she was always writing.

Moving to the closet, Nora saw that it, too, had been emptied. "She sure cleared out fast," Nora muttered. What had sent her running away like this?

Nora lifted the folded papers from the dresser. Curious as ever, she opened the papers and began to read the top page:

Dear Nora,

If you are reading this, then you are already snooping in my things. It is all right. I had counted on it. Forgive me for departing with no parting farewell, but it was at Lord Darlington's insistence. I thank you for your friendliness to me and would like to do something for you in return. My mother was able to afford her flower shop because of the Darlington family, and I think that the least the Darlington family can do is make it possible for you to have your tearoom. At the rate you are going, sewing when you are able, you will be an elderly woman by the time you can afford to achieve your dream. But this satire I have written will help your dream come true much faster.

Yes, your suspicions were correct, I am the author of the satires. But it was not greed that led me to betray the Darlingtons. The satire enclosed here will be my last. And it is my parting gift to you. I believe its contents will explain why I have done what I have. If you take it to them, the Sussex Courier will pay fifty pounds for it. The series has become so popular that if you insist on sixty pounds there is an excellent chance you will get your price.

Good luck to you, my friend. I hope that someday I might return to London and enjoy a cup of tea and a scone at your lovely teahouse.

Therese

So Therese was the author of those scathing satires all the while! Why did she do it? What could possibly have made her despise the Darlingtons so much that she would want to hurt them like that?

It had to have been for the money. But for that, she could have twisted Wesley around her little finger; he was clearly so enamored of her. Yet she hadn't given him the least encouragement. Strange.

Filing the front page to the back, Nora began to read Therese's last satire. As she scanned the handwritten piece, her eyes widened and her jaw went slack with surprise.

THE FURTHER ADVENTURES OF...
THE WORTHLESS SAGA

The Last Rib-Tickling Installment
of our Popular New Series
"What Does Another Heir Matter
When There's Nothing Left to Inherit?"

Anyone who has visited Faded Glory Manor lately has seen the depths to which the Worthless family has tumbled.

Just recently Lady Worthless was seen with her hair disheveled, her collar torn, rocking a bawling baby in her arms. "I'm too old for this!" she shouted as a door fell off its hinges. "I thought I could raise this baby as my own, but I'm simply too antiquated." She pointed to a gilt-framed portrait of one of the Worthless ancestors—a soldier in a doublet and velvet tights—on the wall, dating back to the 1600s. "I'm almost as old as *he* is," she said with a sigh. "At least I feel that way since this baby came along."

Snobby came running in. "How is my little cutesie-bootsie today?" she asks, tickling the baby under the chin.

Lady Worthless shooed Snobby away. "Don't even look at this baby. Someone might notice his resemblance to you and to a certain someone."

Snobby looked away from her mother. "I

can't imagine what you might mean by that, Mother," she said with mock sincerity.

"You understand full well what I mean," Lady Worthless insisted.

"I assure you, I do not," Snobby replied.

"Can I remind you of a few months back when your belly looked as if you'd swallowed a melon whole," Lady Worthless retorted.

Snobby stuck a finger in either ear. "I can't hear you!" she sung out.

Lady Worthless stamped her foot in frustration. "Oh! You make me so mad! You are just like your father!"

"My father?" Snobby gasped. "In what manner could I possibly resemble that blustering old coot?"

"Well, you both have a child that you won't admit to!"

"Shh!!!!" Snobby hissed sharply. "What child won't father admit is his? Doodles?"

Doodles rushed in. "I'm not father's child?" she asked, aghast.

"Shh!" Lady Worthless and Snobby shushed her at once. "No, not you, Doodles, silly girl," said Lady Worthless. "The nanny."

"The nanny?!" Doodles and Snobby cried in one voice. "The nanny is a Worthless?"

"I'm afraid it's true," Lady Worthless admitted as she continued to bounce the baby. "Years ago Lord Worthless dallied with Nanny's mother, who was a very young maid in the household. They sent her off to France and paid her never to return."

Abby Grahame

"But she did return?" Doodles asked.

"The child grew up to be Nanny and she came back to claim her inheritance. She fooled us all by pretending to be poor."

"But she is poor," Snobby reminded her mother. "Everyone who works for us is poor because we pay them hardly anything."

"I suppose that's so," Lady Worthless agreed as a slab of ceiling crashes to the floor at her feet.

"Are you telling us we have a poor relative?" Doodles asked in horror.

"Shh!" Lady Worthless said again. She lowers her voice. "That's why your father wouldn't admit to having a child by a maid. It's so embarrassing to know poor people, let alone be so . . . familiar . . . with one."

"But Mother, aren't we poor now?" Snobby asked.

"Shh!" said Lady Worthless. "We are not poor. We're impecunious."

"What does that mean?" Doodles asked.

"Poor," Snobby filled her in.

"No! No!" Lady Worthless objected. "We're penniless but not poor. We still have the Worthless name, which is worth its weight in gold."

"A name weighs nothing," Doodles said.

"Exactly!" said Lady Worthless.

Snobby scratched her head in bewilderment. "So how does that make me like Father?"

"You dolt!" Lady Worthless cried. "You both have a child you won't admit is yours."

"Snobby has a child?!" Doodles cried.

"Shh!" hissed Snobby.

At that moment Jon Handsome, the stable boy, stomps in, leaving muddy boot prints on the floor. He snaps the straps of his overalls and lifts the baby out of Lady Worthless's arms, letting his feet dangle in the air. "There's my darling son," he said proudly. "He looks just like me, don't you think?"

"Hush!" said Snobby. "He most certainly does not!"

"Sure he does," Jon insisted. "He's lucky. I'm a good-looking fellow. At least that's what you told me that night in the stable. Don't you remember?"

"You must be thinking of someone else," Snobby insisted.

"No, I'm not. It was you all right!"

"You win! He is our baby. Now the whole county will know," Snobby said. "If we raise him as a Worthless, though, he will inherit the Worthless fortune."

"You don't have to worry about that," said Lady Worthless. "Here in this safe is our fortune." She went to the portrait of her ancestor in the velvet tights and lifts it off the wall. Behind it is a safe, which she opens.

Everyone said "Ahh" as a single brown moth flew out of the empty safe.

Nora stopped reading and shook her head, stunned by the information revealed in the satire. She knew, of course,

Aby Grahame

about Maggie and Michael. But that Therese was Lord Darlington's daughter!

What luck for the Darlingtons that this never got published! Therese must have been so furious with her father for the way he denied her that she lashed out at the family any way she could.

Nora ran her eyes along the page once more. It was cruel and unfair to the girls and Lady Darlington, as well as Michael and the baby. What kind of mind could judge good people so harshly, though she had to admit that Lord Darlington probably deserved everything he got. How ironic that the daughter he wouldn't acknowledge was the one who had turned out to be most like him.

Fifty pounds was a lot of money. It would take her years of sewing to earn as much. With a deep sigh of regret, Nora tore the pages in half and then in half again before tossing them in the trash basket. "Fifty pounds down the drain," she murmured, shaking her head woefully.

Nora hurried down the stairs to the kitchen. "Have you seen Michael?" she asked Rose, the cook.

"Not in the last hour," Rose responded. "Why are you looking for him?"

"I just need to speak to him," Nora brushed her off as she headed for the back door. She crossed to the stable and entered. "Michael? Are you in here?"

A horse nickered in response to Nora's voice.

"Michael?" Nora tried again.

He wasn't there, but he always worked at this time. Where could he have gone?

A great silence welled up just behind the soft shuffling of hoofs and occasional sputter of a horse. "Michael?" Nora tried again more softly, now suspecting that Michael might never respond.

Everything was changing. She could feel it and it gave her a chill. But another emotion ran through her. A deep instinct told her that the end of Wentworth Hall had somehow begun. The life of being a serving person on this once great estate—the colorless life she had, deep down, always assumed would be hers—would never be the same. This life was ending and a new one was opening up before her.

Everything was changing. Nora could feel it. And she was glad.

Chapter Twenty-Three

MAGGIE PUSHED HER WINDBLOWN HAIR from her eyes and gazed out across the glistening ocean. She could hardly believe she was on a ship bound for America. Reaching out, she gripped Michael's warm, strong hand and smiled up at James, peacefully asleep on his shoulder.

"Is this really happening?" Maggie asked him.

"It's happening," Michael confirmed with a warm smile. "And it's exactly what *should* be happening. Nothing has ever felt as right to me in my entire life."

Maggie squeezed his hand lovingly, knowing that it was true and deriving strength from his confidence. Maybe some might consider what she was doing wrong. But nothing had felt so right in ages.

In America, no one would care if she was a Darlington. It would be neither an honor nor a disgrace. She would simply be Maggie, her own self.

Michael drew her close to him and wrapped her in his free arm. Maggie rested her head on his chest, letting the drumming of his heartbeat merge with the crash of the waves. "I love you," she said.

"I love you, too. And I love the baby. We're going to be happy, Maggie."

Epilogue

SEVERAL MONTHS LATER, MAGGIE HELD
James in her arms as she leaned against a doorjamb
in their New York apartment. The little fellow's eyes
were drifting shut. He'd had an exciting day in the park,
now that he'd learned to take a few steps. He was happily
exhausted. In her free hand, she held a letter from Lila giving her news of Wentworth Hall and her family.

She couldn't believe nearly a year had passed since she
and Michael had come to America. What an adventure it
had been at first! How happy they were now that they'd
finally moved into their own place.

To think, too, that it was Lila who had struck on this
plan. Lila, who she thought she'd had to protect, had ended

up saving her. Of course Ian had been wonderful too. It was so sweet of him to let them stay in his family's New York apartment when they first arrived in New York. If it hadn't been for his motorcar they never would have been able to get to the dock and aboard the ship sailing for America. He even lent them the money they needed until Maggie had pawned her jewels and paid him back.

"I don't care a bit!" Maggie had assured Michael when he protested. "They're all old and out of style anyway. Our new, amazing life is worth so much more than a few shiny trinkets."

Michael's first stop was to seek work at Belmont Park racetrack on Long Island, outside the city. There was nothing for him but they told him to check back in a few months. For now he was working as a courier and making enough to support them. He'd even begun talking about opening his own courier business, maybe out on Long Island.

Maggie closed her eyes to let the image of them in a regular house in the country sink in. "We'll be happy," she crooned to the sleeping baby, "in our own home someday soon."

James sighed in his sleep and shifted his position.

Maggie glanced at the letter she held. Lila had reported that she and Ian had stayed in touch after heading back to universty with Wes. He had been invited back to Wentworth Hall to have Christmas with the family. Someday, Maggie dared to hope they might even forgive Michael and her, even though Lord Darlington had disinherited her and James for now.

"I hope someday you'll see your grandparents," Maggie whispered hopefully to James. "Maybe Lila will marry Ian and move to America. Wouldn't that be wonderful!"

Besides, Wesley had been supportive. "Don't fret about being disinherited too much," he'd counseled them. "I've seen the account books. There's no big inheritance coming your way. Lila and I will split whatever we get three ways. I promise."

"Will he disown Lila for this, as well?" Maggie had asked.

Wesley had shaken his head. "He doesn't know this was her bright idea. Or of Ian's role. I certainly won't tell him."

What a crushing week it had been for her father, Maggie considered. The news that she was leaving with

Michael—plus the Fitzhugh twins had left the day of their eighteenth birthdays without even saying good-bye. That potentially lucrative alliance had also crashed and burned before his very eyes.

James stirred on her shoulder and lifted his head. His green eyes opened. The breeze from the open window ruffled his downy tufts of hair, making him smile. Maggie reached up to run her fingertips along his baby-soft cheeks.

Michael walked in from his job and smiled at them, encircling both Maggie and the baby in his arms. "That's right, James, you smile," he spoke to James tenderly. "Mommy and Daddy are here and there are nothing but good days ahead."

Maggie reached up and kissed Michael. Never in her life had she felt more loved and more optimistic about the future. "Good days ahead," she echoed. "Such good days."

ABOUT THE AUTHOR

Abby Grahame lives in upstate New York. Her interest in historical fiction and British period dramas inspired *Wentworth Hall*. This is her first novel.

  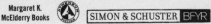